A Vessel Awakens

Book One of the Pantheon War Trilogy

Daniel J. Ward

Pantheon War Trilogy
Book One
A Vessel Awakens

©2018 Daniel J. Ward

ISBN: 978-1-9995409-0-6

Table of Contents

"Dear Uncle Michelle,

I hope the afterlife is treating you well. I appreciate that you thought of me when you wrote your will. Perhaps in your next life you will have the decency to tell me ahead of time how dangerous, and bat shit insane your life is.

All the best,

Domonic."

Chapter One
Rainy Days

"I can't find any of my socks. Seriously? It's like there is some kind of evil little demon that gains sustenance through the act of hiding my shit!" I muttered and hissed at no one in particular. I looked at Coaldust, my cat. He stretched and yawned. "You don't have to worry about socks, right, Coaldust?" I scratched behind his ears while I finished packing.

"Fuck it. I'll wear flip-flops, pack my shoes, and buy socks when I get there!" I said to him. He was a happy little cat, an odd fur ball who liked to go for walks on occasion but was otherwise a lazy guy who liked to sleep, eat, and claw up my shins. His black fur hadn't changed one bit in six years.

My phone rang. It was my parents.

"Hello?" I never knew which one of them would be on the line.

"Hi sweetie, how are you?" My mom sounded really upset. I never liked hearing her like that.

"I'm alright, just getting ready to go to the airport. How are you holding up?" She sniffled. Coaldust heard her voice and meowed up at the phone.

"Coaldust says hi." She loved my little cat quite a bit.

"That's sweet. Your dad is putting our luggage in the car, then we're on our way. I guess we'll see you there. We won't be arriving until the day of the funeral. -zZzzZzZZzzz- Can't wait - ZZzz..zZz.- you dear. -ZZzzz...-" The call connection was terrible.

"Mom? I'll see you there, okay? I love you! Mom? -ZzzZzz..click-click-" I looked at my phone and hung up. I noticed the time, and I was already cutting it closer than I wanted to. Time to go.

"Alright buddy, I'll be back in a few days. Once this funeral is done and over with, we can enjoy our normal rhythm again. Ruth will come by to check on you. She promised to take you on walks so please be nice to her!"

I stopped by Ruth's apartment before I left. She was like a grandmother to me. We had been neighbors for almost six years now. She had no family that I knew of. She had slipped and fallen, breaking her hip, shortly after I moved in. I had helped her a lot through that time, and we enjoyed each other's company. She was family to me now.

I reached up and knocked on her door. I could hear her feet pad toward it, and the lock switch open.

"Hello Dommy, are you leaving now?" She looked down past my legs and took note of my luggage. Her eyebrows raised at the sight of my bare feet in flip-flops. "It's raining out there, you know." The concern was heavy in her voice.

"I can't find any of my socks. I'll be alright though." I reached into my pocket and produced a key to my apartment. "His leash is hanging up behind the door. There's a couple hundred dollars in the tea tin on top of the fridge. You can use that for whatever you want. Food, alcohol, drugs..."

Ruth scoffed and smirked at me. I leaned in and gave her a hug. "Thanks Ruth, I'll let you know when I get there safe and sound."

She squeezed back, then pushed me back and tapped me firmly on the shoulder. "Domonic Anth, you get some socks on those feet right away."

I couldn't help but chuckle, I looked down and wiggled my toes.

"I will, thank you, Ruth!" I grabbed my luggage and was on my way.

I knew it was going to be a good trip. It was raining. It always rained when I took a plane. On this day it was just pouring. By the time they called for boarding, it had eased up quite a bit. There was a total knockout of a stewardess who kept checking on me early in the flight; brown hair, full lips, and a wonderful figure. It was a long flight from Seattle to Baltimore - my plan was to sleep the whole way. It took a while to fall asleep, but when I did, I dreamt of the stewardess. She looked like Nicole in my dream. We had finally been ready to go out on an honest-to-goodness date, and then the funeral happened.

At the time, I wasn't looking forward to flying to Baltimore. The funeral was for my Uncle Michelle, and I hadn't seen him in just about twenty years. I didn't think there was much choice in the matter though. He had been thoughtful enough to put me in his will and had requested that I be present at his funeral. I didn't know if he had any other family, or what I was being given in his will. I had never been in someone's will... and if I had known what I was about to receive, I would have wished for it to stay that way.

When I landed in Baltimore, I realized that departures get all the good restaurants, and arrivals get much less. My stomach gurgled with hunger. I gathered my luggage at the carousel, then proceeded to the exit to find a cab. On my way out, I found a sharply dressed black man standing patiently, holding a sign with "*Mr. Anth*" on it. The suit he was wearing looked far more expensive than any of the clothes I owned. He was tall, black, and had a short, neat hairstyle. He looked like he was somewhere between 30 and 40 years old. I approached him.

"Excuse me, that's my name, but I didn't arrange for a car..."

The man looked pleased to see me and put the sign away.

"No sir, I was sent by Mr. Donovan. He instructed me to give you this envelope."

I knew Mr. Donovan. He was the lawyer handling the will. I opened the envelope and pulled out a note.

"Dear Mr. Anth, the man handing you this letter is Carl. He will help you reach me safely. Do join him, and feel free to help yourself to anything you like in the car."

I nodded as I read. The letterhead was from Mr. Donovan's offices. I tucked the letter away and shrugged, letting Carl lead me to the car. He looked satisfied and motioned for me to follow him. He led me to a beautiful black Town Car, opened the back door for me, and was kind enough to put my luggage in the trunk for me.

I climbed into the back seat. It was roomy enough that I could make myself very comfortable. There was a small bar area along the back edge of the driver's seat, where I found five unmarked crystal decanters. Three were filled about half way with a brown liquid, and the other two with a clear liquid. Two highball glasses were set into clips on a small red velvet shelf.

"So, Carl, how long of a drive is it?" I asked as he settled in his seat.

"There has been a change of location sir. Mr. Donovan is in Cape Charles at the moment, and we will be meeting him there. I believe it is about four hours away."

I would definitely be drinking from those decanters.

"Hey Carl, I don't want to be a bother, but on the way if you see some place I can buy socks, I'd appreciate the stop - and maybe a quick bite to eat."

Carl chuckled as he adjusted his mirrors. "Sir, we can stop wherever you want, for however long you want."

I thought about it for a moment. "First, I need to get some socks, and then I need food." Carl nodded, and we were off.

It wasn't long before he pulled into a parking lot. He turned over his shoulder to look at me. "Sir, what size of shoes do you wear?"

I looked down at my flip flops, and then back to him. "Thirteen, wide."

Before I could protest, Carl had hopped out of the car and headed into a shop. He came back a few minutes later with a dozen socks, handed them to me over the seat, and then we were back on the road.

"Carl, I could have went in and gotten them."

He waved his hand at me dismissively. "No, sir. I will be reimbursed by Mr. Donovan."

Shortly after that, we pulled up to a drive-thru. We called out our orders and in a couple minutes we were parked off the road, eating. I had a burger and a milkshake. Carl had a large fry, and a Sprite.

After we had eaten and were driving again, I tried a little splash from each of the decanters - bourbon, blended whiskey, vodka, something I couldn't put my finger on, and water. It was strange to me that someone would keep a bunch of liquor in their car, but who was I to judge?

It occurred to me that I should let my parents know of the venue change. I had been under the impression that the service and wake were going to be in Baltimore. I dialed my mother's cell phone.

"The number you are trying to reach is unavailable."

I gathered they were probably in the air still. I tried my father's cell phone. He had voicemail and neither of them liked to text.

"Hi, you've reached Mark and Eireen. Please leave a message after the beep."

I cleared my throat waiting for the beep.

-beep-

"Hey Dad, they moved the service to Cape Charles. It's about 4 hours from Baltimore. When you get this voicemail, call me back please. Love you guys." I hung up the call and went back to looking out the window.

It was dark and raining when we pulled up to a beach house. I was already pretty tired, but the excitement of arriving had woken me up a little. It felt good to get out and stretch.

"Thanks for the ride, Carl." I took my luggage out of the trunk.

He closed the lid. "Thank you for the food Mr. Anth."

I waved it off. "You're welcome, and call me Domonic. Mr. Anth feels way too formal."

The front door to the beach house opened and an older man called out. "Carl! Is that Mr. Anth? If so send him in, enough standing in the rain!"

I looked to Carl. "Mr. Donovan?"

Carl nodded.

I raised my eyebrows as I turned and made my way up to the house. The rain got more intense, falling harder and louder with every step. I loved it. I have always loved the rain.

I entered Mr. Donovan's house, and was greeted by a man who looked and sounded just like Brian Cox. He stood there in an evening robe with a drink in each hand.

"Well-well, you look the part of a drowned rat, Mr. Anth! I have been eager to meet you since we spoke on the phone, and I must say, you are taller than I thought you would be. I'm Eric Donovan."

I took the drink he offered and noticed he wasn't wearing his shoes in the house, so I kicked mine off and followed him upstairs.

"Mr. Anth, you'll be staying in one of the rooms down the hall here - take any room you want. Your parents will be staying here as well when they arrive. When you're ready and settled, come down to the lounge and have a drink!"

I watched him walk away. "If this day gets any weirder, I'll need more than one." I muttered to myself.

I walked down the hall and found an open door. Inside was a modest room with a twin bed and some free desk space. I was impressed to find that it had its own bathroom. I finished my drink and took the opportunity to shower and put on a dry change of clothes. Feeling renewed from the warm shower, I made my way to the lounge to see what Mr. Donovan wanted.

I entered the room to see Mr. Donovan filling two glasses with dark red wine from a crystal decanter. The room was warmer than normal; a gas fireplace was pumping out a surprising amount of heat. There were incredibly comfortable-looking chairs set up in front of the fireplace and the room was darker than the other rooms I had been to so far. The ambience was perfect for a relaxing evening. Mr. Donovan came over and offered me a glass. I took it and thanked him. I normally didn't like wine, but I didn't want to be rude. I sipped it tentatively and was pleasantly surprised. It was far better than anything I had ever had before.

"Thank you, Mr. Donovan. Have you spoken to my parents? I haven't been able to reach them."

I continued to sip away while Mr. Donovan went to a bookshelf and pulled a large metal box from one of the shelves. He motioned for me to sit.

"You are welcome. Your parents? I spoke with them yesterday - I had to let them know about the change of location for the funeral." He paused and thoughtfully looked from his glass to me. "How do you like the wine? It's from the greatest vineyard in the universe!" Mr. Donovan stifled a laugh.

"Oh, it's amazing! I'm not a big wine drinker, but this stuff is really great."

He shuffled over towards me, carrying the metal box. "Your uncle Michelle had been a client of mine for 34 years. I didn't know it when he first walked into my office, but he is - or was rather -

a very wealthy man. I wouldn't have guessed it though. He had on plain brown slacks and a flannel-patterned button-up shirt. I suppose that's neither here nor there though. I was specifically instructed to go through some things with you before the official reading of the will after his funeral" He paused, patting his bathrobe pockets. "Just a moment... I have left the key upstairs."

Mr. Donovan left the lounge and I looked at the metal box with curiosity. I hadn't seen my uncle in many years, but in my last memory of him, he wore comfortable clothes and drove a beat-up station wagon. He didn't ever give the impression that he was well off.

Mr. Donovan had been gone for only a few minutes when the lightning and thunder started. When he returned, the rain was noisily raking across the windows even harder than before.

"Here we are!" He sat back down and worked through his keyring. "Now, I know this isn't the formal reading, but the funeral is tomorrow and by then the others will all be here." He looked a little frustrated. "I was instructed to give you the contents of this lockbox before the reading."

Mr. Donovan set the lockbox in the middle of the table and motioned for me to join him. I sat beside him and watched as he chose an old brass key, marked with dark scratches and dents. It carried age in its patina. He removed it from his keyring, and held it out to me, looking amused.

"I must confess, shortly before you arrived, I had the box up in my room. I tried to get it open so I could present you with the contents and an itemized list. I tried and tried to get that key to turn, but it doesn't budge." He laughed, mostly out of frustration I'm sure.

I took the key and turned it around in my hand. I looked at the lockbox, slid the key into the lock, and tried to turn it. No luck for me either. I looked at the keyhole and tried turning the key around. The back end of the key fit in the keyhole too, and still it would not turn. I sighed and tossed the key on the table and took a long drink of my wine.
"Well that's… fun, I guess."

Mr. Donovan chuckled and nodded. "Well I suppose you'll have to deal with that lock in your own time."

We sat for a while listening to the sound of the rain. After I finished my wine, I felt my eyelids grow heavy. It was time for bed.

"Mr. Donovan, I think it's time for sleep!" I said, standing.

He leaned over to grab the wine bottle and refilled his glass. "Have a wonderful rest, see you in the morning."

I picked up the lock box and headed up to my room. I could feel something odd on the underside of the box as I carried it. I lifted it up to peer underneath and saw a bunch of oddly-shaped holes covering the bottom of it. Weird triangles were stamped into the corners as well. I sighed to myself, not knowing what to do about the box, and not really caring at the moment. It would be a deep sleep that night. The flight had exhausted me, and the wine wasn't helping.

Back in my room, I took a minute to gaze out the window. The view was of the water. Choppy grey skies mirrored the turbulent ocean below. I laid down with the lockbox beside me. The bed was softer than I had expected, and I fell asleep quickly, thinking about the holes, and about the lock.

The next morning, I was awakened by the smell of cooking bacon... and wine? I looked at my bedside table and there was my wine glass. I didn't remember bringing it upstairs with me. "Huh, I thought I…"

Suddenly I was dizzy. I felt sick to my stomach. I dashed to the bathroom and threw up a surprising volume of red liquid. It must have been the wine. At least it tasted like wine - wine and vomit. After a few more heaves, I felt much better. I flushed the toilet and watched the red swirls disappear.

I cleaned myself up and made my way downstairs to find a simple breakfast of bacon and eggs. Mr. Donovan whistled and shuffled his feet as he cooked.

"Good morning! I thought you would like something for breakfast!"

I squinted and smiled tightly as I took a seat. There was a cup of strong black coffee sitting on the table, which I helped myself to.

I coughed and sputtered.

"Ah, I forgot to mention, there is whiskey in that coffee."

I couldn't believe this man was a lawyer.

"Any other surprises I should be aware of?" I took another sip of the coffee, appreciating the soothing bite of the whiskey.

"Surprises? No... nothing comes to mind. But I guess we'll see what the will says."

I paused and looked at him over my shoulder before asking. "You don't know what's in the will?"

Mr. Donovan sheepishly turned away from the bacon and looked at me. "I don't. Your uncle had the will drawn up elsewhere, and then asked me to be the one to ensure it is read and handled. Although he did tell me a few things that I would find in there. Like your lockbox."

It seemed strange to me, but who was I to argue with the will of a dead man. "Fair enough, thanks for breakfast, and the uh... coffee."

~

"Michelle Hethenal Tennant was an eccentric man, but he was kind, generous, and he trusted in the goodness of the heart of all people. He left behind no family of his own, although he did have many friends, as you can see from how many are present." Hundreds of people nodded along, some smiled at each other, while others gently wept. "Michelle was born in St. Johns, Ontario, Canada in 1953 on April first. His mother was from Paris, France and his father was from Athens, Greece. Michelle was a darling child who was adored by many. Growing up, he achieved excellence in his education and spent his days living in luxury. He excelled at philanthropic investments. He will be missed by many, for he changed the lives of many. Goodbye Michelle. We all love you very much."

Carl paused. Backing away from the microphone, he pulled a tissue from his pocket and gently wiped his eyes. He took a moment to compose himself and returned to the mic.

"Now, if you would please stay seated, there is a song Michelle wanted you to hear today."

The sound of a lone feminine voice pierced through the air, catching the attention of everyone in attendance. We all looked around, trying to figure out where the singing was coming from. She strode out slowly from behind a purple curtain. She was petite, maybe 5'1, and had shoulder-length blonde hair that fell in curls just past her shoulders. She wore a black dress, which did not make it very far down her legs, and her lips were softened with a pink shade of lipstick. I was immediately attracted to her, a sentiment likely shared with most of the men in the room. Her singing was beautiful. It felt otherworldly. Her voice faded to silence, and the crowd remained in a hush.

Mr. Donovan walked up to the mic. She bowed slightly and stepped behind the curtain again.

"Michelle had nothing else planned." Mr. Donovan's voice broke the singer's sirens' hold. "There is a buffet available for everyone to enjoy. Those whom I contacted regarding his will, please follow me."

And with that, Mr. Donovan left through a side door. A few others and I followed. I looked around, trying to find my parents, but they were nowhere to be seen. Passing through the door behind Mr. Donovan, I noticed that the blonde singer was in the office as well. Feeling brave, I approached her.

"Hi, my name is…"

"There will be time for that later, let's get this will reading done." Mr. Donovan interrupted me with impeccable timing. "It's not very long, relatively simple in fact. Everyone gets something. Let's figure out what that is."

I was irritated by Mr. Donovan's interruption. It couldn't have been deliberate, yet I felt like it was.

Everyone nodded and took a seat. The blonde smiled at me with a coy look in her eyes. I needed to know her name.

"Alright, here we are. Just a few moments… Seems there is only one clause. It all goes to a variety of charities in the event that his nephew is dead - thankfully for everyone here he is not."

Mr. Donovan motioned towards me and the others glanced my way.

"Alright, first off. 'Dear Mr. Donovan, you are being gifted ten thousand dollars every month for ten years, totalling one million two hundred thousand dollars. This is contingent on the condition that you provide yourself to my nephew at all times for any legal issues he may have over the next decade.' Hmmm... this goes on for a while talking about legal fees and a trust account. It appears that if you ever run into trouble, you only need to call me, and I'm supposed to get you out of it." He looked pointedly at me. "Try to stay out of trouble."

Everyone chuckled at that. I exhaled heavily out of my nose and smiled.

"'Next, to everyone present, with the exception of my nephew and Mr. Donovan, I leave one million dollars for each of your respective charities. Additionally, you each personally receive an additional five hundred thousand dollars.' He left a small note here."

"'*Thank you all for your help over these long years. I appreciate your discretion in this matter. Lastly, I leave to you all the gift of my nephew. Look upon him, for he shall take my place.*'"

Everyone looked at me with wide eyes, and suddenly I didn't know if I liked what I was hearing. Mr. Donovan cleared his throat.

"Domonic, he has a message for you as well."

"'*My dear nephew. I loved seeing you as a child. Your sense of wonder and your inquisitive mind always made me appreciate how fragile and precious innocence is, and why it must be cherished. I leave to you my properties, my possessions, investment accounts, liquid assets, and trust funds totaling one hundred and thirty five million dollars. You will have immediate and unlimited access to twenty five million dollars. The remainder has been arranged to ensure that your bank account receives funds every month, and to cover expenses incurred by your new properties.*"

I was stunned. I couldn't accept what I had just heard. Everyone was looking at me.

Before I had time to process, Mr. Donovan pulled out a stack of documents. It took some time for him to go over them with everyone, asking for signatures and signing himself as witness. He saved mine for last. I appreciated it. The others all left after signing their documents, and finally it came to me. I still didn't know exactly how to handle what I had just heard.

"Are you alright?" Mr. Donovan looked at me with a mix of humor and concern.

I was still processing what was happening.

"Mr. Anth, are you okay?"

I watched him stand and pour himself a drink, and started to wonder… "Hey, Mr. Donovan, why is there liquor here? And why are you in an office at a funeral home?"

He put the lid back on whatever he was pouring and turned to me. "Well, I asked if I could make use of their office, since mine is four hours away. As for the liquor… I don't know, but I believe you could find out from someone who works here. I figure it is fair game, not being locked in a cabinet." He grinned and unscrewed the top.

I didn't question him further.

I started to get a grip of myself while Mr. Donovan enjoyed his drink. I focused on the sound of the rain beating against the window.

"Let's go over the paperwork, shall we…?" Mr. Donovan motioned for me to take a seat closer to the desk. I moved to where he had indicated

I started to realize that I could quit working day jobs and pursue whatever I wanted.

"Now, there are a couple things here I was supposed to avoid bringing up until you and I were alone. First, all of this wealth and property is yours, but there is a condition. You must call and quit your job right now. And you can't tell anyone why." He pushed the landline towards me.

I looked at him and obediently took the receiver. I fished out my cell phone with the other hand and searched my contacts for my supervisor's number.

I took out my phone and dialed Kyle. The second I heard it ring, I immediately felt sick to my stomach. What was I doing? I didn't want to do this to Kyle, we had been friends for years before we started working together. He was like a brother to me. My head pounded and my heart ached.

ring ring

ring ring

"I.T. In Reach Outsourcing, Kyle speaking, how can I help you?"

I hated myself as soon as the words started to leave my mouth.

"Kyle, hey man, how you doing? I have to uh… quit. Today. I can't talk - I am in Baltimore, and I just - have to do this. So, uh yeah, that's all... and... Please send any paperwork you need to my home address...."

I waited for a response from him…. Nothing. Before the phone went down I caught some of what he said though. "Fucking asshole." *click*

Mr. Donovan nodded and pushed some papers at me. "Take your time. Read it all. If you have any questions let me know."

I went through it all slowly, several times. I was going to be filthy rich, rich enough to do anything I wanted. It was incredible.

After signing the documents, Mr. Donovan poured me a drink. I didn't even taste it. I was electric with energy and I couldn't feel anything other than excitement.

"Now that everything is settled here, it'll take a few days for the banks to move everything around. I'll get the properties transferred to your name - and this is yours." He handed me a cashier's cheque for fifty thousand dollars.

"Your uncle arranged for you to have it for immediate use."

Mr. Donovan continued to organize and prepare documents for me while I sat listening in stunned silence.

"Oh! And just one more thing... The beach house we're staying in used to be your uncle's. He gave it to me as part of payment for my services. I'd like you to take a key and feel free to use it whenever you need. I will be there a few times a month, maybe for weekends, but feel free to come around!"

I nodded and took the key with the intention of adding it to my current collection of keys, but all I could do was stare. My eyes landed on my parent's house keys. Where were they? I started to feel uneasy.

"That's fine, Mr. Donovan, I appreciate the offer. I just need to make another phone call. I didn't see my parents out there."

I took deep breath. I didn't know how they were going to react to the news about the inheritance. Mr. Donovan nodded, handing me the cashier's cheque.

I called my father's phone again. It went straight to voicemail *"Hi you've reached Mark and Eireen. Please leave a message after the beep."*

I sighed and waited for the beep.

-beep-

"Hey Dad, didn't see you or mom here at the funeral. I have some big news. Can you call me when you get this message, or just delete this if I see you before you get this. Love you."

Mr. Donovan was looking outside at the seemingly perpetual storm clouds. He turned back to me. "Mark and Eireen, I haven't seen them in... years! Not since I did their wills!" He leaned against the window and crossed his arms. "I would bet their plane was routed to another airport. All up and down the East Coast has been hit with storms the last couple of weeks."

He's probably right. It makes sense.

I rubbed my hands on my knees. Despite what I told myself, I felt a tremendous amount of butterflies in my stomach.

"I guess you're my lawyer now too. We should probably get to know each other."

Mr. Donovan filled two glasses with whatever was in the cheap looking bottle of liquor, and he passed one to me.

"For the next ten years, at least! Then you'll need to sign another contract with new terms if you want to continue the arrangement."

He chuckled and raised his glass. I raised mine to him, and we drank. He cleared his throat. "Now then, it's time to finish up this paperwork!"

There were a few more papers to sign, then we were finished in the office and left to join the others.

I tried very hard not to look as giddy as I felt. When I arrived at the buffet with Mr. Donovan, there was music and alcohol and a lot of food. I picked out some of the food and piled it on a paper plate, helped myself to a water bottle, and walked around looking at the plants. I didn't know anyone here and wasn't interested in making friends. I looked around for my parents, but they were still not here.

After an hour or so, Mr. Donovan pulled out a microphone and tapped to check it was working.

"Alright everyone, I hope you have finished mourning here. It is currently 4:00 pm. The next phase of the funeral is at King's Creek Resort. Wine will be served there. The party, or wake if you prefer, starts at 8:00 pm. Please take some time to freshen up, and I'll see you all there!"

Everyone raised their glasses to Mr. Donovan. No one seemed perturbed by his seemingly carefree approach to my uncle's funeral.

On our way back to the beach house, I stopped by my bank branch to deposit my cashier's cheque. I spent an hour with Mr. Donovan and the branch manager going through paperwork before we headed back to the beach house to get changed.

"I suppose I should start figuring out what to do with myself."

There was a long silence before Mr. Donovan cleared his throat and walked down the hall toward me. He dropped his hands firmly on my shoulders and gently shook me.

"You're rich lad, you do whatever the hell you want!" He squeezed my shoulders amiably, then turned and strode down the hall to his room, laughing.

I looked at my phone. I had just over an hour left before we needed to leave for the wake.

It was taking some time to set in, but he was right. I was rich! I had more money at that very moment than I had ever had at one time in my life. I opened up my banking app and checked my balance. $58,943.22. I could also see a list of nine more accounts that were status pending. Over the next week I was going to see some really big numbers start showing up in there. I wished I had taken notes. I couldn't believe this was happening, and I wasn't sure how to keep it all straight. I was used to one bank account with very little in it.

I looked at the lockbox and couldn't imagine what was inside of it. Treasure? Jewels? I supposed it didn't really matter.

I sat on the bed, partially dressed, and suddenly felt very heavy. I had no significant memories of my uncle, and now he was gone. Somehow, he had seen fit to leave me a vast amount of wealth. I had no idea what to do with it, or with myself. I felt profoundly sad and guilty that I hadn't gotten to know him better and felt a sudden burning rage at Mr. Donovan. His words from the funeral dug at my mind *"Alright everyone, I hope you have finished mourning here."* Such callous words and disregard. I was red in the neck from it. I got up to go confront him - and froze.

I was shocked to find that I had a rock-hard erection. I closed the door quickly, looking down and wondering where this had come from.

"What the fuck is this? This… This is… oh, wow!"

I gasped. There was a heat against my neck. It felt like warm breath running from my collarbone to my ear, and back again. My nose caught the scent of faint smoke. My ears throbbed with a high-pitched ringing. As it faded, I felt an overwhelming need to get out of my clothes and I quickly pulled them off. It felt like someone was helping me. I fell to the bed, naked, a pressure on my wrists like hands were wrapped around them, pressing me down into the bed. I audibly moaned as I felt teeth rake my nipples. The sensation made me spasm. I heard a distant echo of some giggling. My eyes closed, and I gave in to what was happening. My body shivered as faint kisses started working down my neck, continuing down my abdomen. The weight left my wrists and the kisses stopped. I thought I felt a faint tickling travelling farther down my body. I opened my eyes and looked down - but no one was there. I closed my eyes tightly again and the pressure started to move. Suddenly, I felt a warm mouth... and a tongue. I gasped, reeling with pleasure. The warmth disappeared, the pressure shifted, and I felt a new warmth. I could feel every movement of another person, the weight of another on my hips. It was amazing, and terrifying. I was close to climax. I groaned, and my jaw clenched in anticipation...

Suddenly, and without warning, everything stopped.

What?

I unconsciously pouted my lips for a second and heard a faint whisper pass by my ears.

"Soon..."

The implication raised more than my spirits, but only for a moment. Without warning, the world came rushing back to me, crashing around my senses. I sat up and looked around the room, then stood.

"What. The. Fuck."

I had no idea what I just experienced. Was it a
dream? Whether it was or not, it suddenly didn't
matter as the strength drained from my body. I
was struck by overwhelming emotions that I
didn't understand, and broke into a fit of
desperate crying. I moved to get up, as if to
escape these foreign emotions, but my knees
buckled underneath me and I fell to the floor,
sobbing. The room felt cold and my head swam
with dizziness. For what felt like an eternity, my
shoulders heaved and my breath shuddered. I
was exhausted, weak, and barely able to move.
Darkness swept over my vision as I passed out
on the floor.

My eyes opened. It took several moments for
me to remember where I was. I tried to compose
myself. It was very hard to do, but not
impossible. It had been only ten or fifteen
minutes since I came to my room, according to
the clock on the bedside table.

I pulled myself up off the floor, and stumbled
into the shower. As the warm water ran over
me, I took my time to breathe and relax. I felt
increasingly better as the minutes went by.
There had been nothing in my life that had ever
terrified or aroused me as much as this had. I
didn't know if I liked what had happened, and I

felt like I needed a hug. I thought of Nicole, of her arms wrapped around me. I loved how she made me feel when I was with her, the way her easy smile made me smile. Thinking of her washed away the lingering sensations from my experience, until it almost seemed like it never happened. Feeling better, I turned off the shower and grabbed a towel from a nearby rack. I dried as I went back to the room and put on my clothes. Still, I felt fine. What had just happened?

I could hear Mr. Donovan leaving his room. He would be waiting for me. I started trying to come up with an excuse for taking so long, and left my room for the wake.

Chapter Two
Unrealistic Expectations

We left the beach house, and I was surprised to see Carl waiting outside with the car. I waved and smiled. He nodded as he opened the door for me.

"There you are, sir," he said, closing the car door behind me and running to the other side to do the same for Mr. Donovan. Carl was purely professional now. He didn't seem like the same guy who had picked me up at the airport. It dawned on me that Mr. Donovan's presence might the reason he was so rigid now.

As Carl drove, Mr. Donovan spent the drive focused on his phone. I looked out the window, catching glimpses of the houses we passed. As we approached, I could see the massive resort and a marina filled with an assortment of boats. I had never spent much time on any watercraft. My dad loved sailing and always talked about taking me one day. Now, I would be able to take him. Maybe I could even get him his own boat! We could go on a real adventure together. I grinned to myself, thinking how excited he would be.

Small raindrops fell on the windshield, and the clouds hinted of rain as we approached the parking area. I saw guests heading in and out of the resort condos. It looked like there were more people here than at the funeral. I had always liked a good party, and I looked forward to it especially now, since it would distract me from the events that had occurred less than an hour ago.

We parked in front of the check-in house. Carl came around and opened our doors. Music echoed around the resort. It appeared the rain had let up enough to enjoy the evening. This was going to be good.

"Carl you should come and join us," I offered. I had trouble seeing him as just a driver. I was growing fond of him, and he was the closest thing I had to a friend here.

Carl shook his head and leaned against the car.

"I'll be along shortly - I just need a few minutes." He pulled out his phone.

Mr. Donovan quickly jumped in and ushered me toward the resort. "I wouldn't worry about Carl.

He is probably just working on impressing you now that you're his employer."

I was flummoxed. "What? I thought Carl was *your* driver…?"

With an awkward chortle of a laugh, Mr. Donovan patted me on the back. "Ah, well, Carl is your employee, along with some other people who your uncle employed to take care of his properties. You'll have time to sort through all of that later. Right now, you need to rub elbows with some of your uncle's old acquaintances. It's bound to be a delightful night."

I looked around the resort. Condos and villas lined the edge of the water, connected by a long winding pathway that led out to some of the docked boats. I could see a small check-in house and a restaurant in the distance. Immediately in front of us were huge tents open on a green space. Under the tents, people were talking, drinking, and having a good time. Mr. Donovan escorted me through the crowd of people and tables. Everyone I passed looked at me and nodded. Some hands reached out for quick shakes. No one offered a name, but they all seemed to know me.

We crossed to the far side of the green space, to a table at the front of the gathering. There were only two seats at this table, with a microphone sitting between them.

"Is this us?"

Mr. Donovan nodded and moved to his seat, and I took mine. He waved at the DJ, and the music stopped. He grabbed the microphone off the table.

"Thank you, everyone. Thank you, esteemed guests, for travelling so far to be with us tonight. There are a few who couldn't be here tonight: I have these words from them.

"Friends, we mourn the passing of a great man. A man who impacted all of our existences and was important to each and every one of us. I can't tell you how much I will miss him personally, and even though we can't be there with you right now, we are thinking of each and every one of you."

Mr. Donovan set a small letter down on the table. Smiling, he motioned towards me.

"Sitting next to me tonight, is the man who has inherited Mr. Tennant's life's work. It is my pleasure to introduce you to his nephew, Domonic Anth."

Everyone clapped softly. More than a few raised their drinks towards me. I didn't know why they were interested in me. Of the few funerals I had been to, no one ever clapped and cheered, and it felt off to me. I stood and waved, feeling like it was the thing to do, but I was embarrassed and uncomfortable.

A thin, handsome man sauntered up. He gently placed an old looking bottle of wine on the table, then reached into his pocket and pulled out a silver ring. He turned it slowly between his fingers, then leaned over the table and set it in front of me. He took his time speaking.

"This ring was a gift I gave to your uncle. He sent it back to me when he knew he was going to pass. I want you to have it now, and this wine, this is yours too. Enjoy it." He paused and thoughtfully looked me in the eyes.

"I will miss Michelle very much."

I picked up the ring and the wine. I couldn't read the label. It was too old and faded. The top had a wax and twine seal over it.

"Thank you! I'm not much of a wine drinker, but this looks… awesome. Thank you."

He watched as I examined the ring. It was beautiful; the inner surfaces were very smooth, and it had a detailed leafy vine engraved into that looked like a grape vine, which wrapped around its entire face. It almost looked alive when I stared at at, as though a breeze might blow by and shake the leaves. I slid the ring onto my left middle finger. It fit perfectly, and felt cool and smooth against my skin.

The man smiled - a warm and inviting smile, confident and knowing. When he finally turned away, he threw his arms up in the air, and the crowd responded by clapping and cheering.

The applause ended quickly, and they were quiet again. I still didn't understand. The applause, the gifts - this wasn't normal.

The crowd was looking at me expectantly. I looked at Mr. Donovan. He moved towards me and leaned in, speaking softly. "It's your turn." He pushed the mic over to me.

I stood. "Hi. I didn't know I'd be making a speech tonight. I didn't really know Uncle Michelle very well and I… well... thanks for being here. I'm sure it would mean a lot to my uncle to know that you came and..."

A sudden feeling of warmth rushing into my head and burning on my hand distracted me from my awkward speech. I looked at the ring on my hand, and I felt myself starting to get dizzy. I reached down and took a sip from my drink - *when did I get a drink?* - to steel my nerves.

And the world faded to darkness.

It has taken some time for the memory to come back to me. I can describe it to you now, although at the time it was lost to me.

The ring on my finger heated up with intensity. I felt a numbing sensation creep over my mind. It felt as if I pulled away from myself. I lost control, and I could only observe as words poured from my mouth that were not my own. Had someone spiked my drink?

My body stepped up to the microphone, ready to speak.

"Friends, thank you for being here. I know we are going to have a great time. My dear sweet nephew," My body touched its chest with both

hands. "He knows not what he has inherited!
Treat him well, and be... be gentle." My face
smiled at the room, but it also felt like it smiled
at me. "Farewell!"

As soon the words stopped, I could feel myself
gaining control again. The music started back
up, and I found my seat. Most of the people in
attendance had begun to mingle and drink. I sat
there for a little while, wondering what had
happened. I couldn't make sense of it.

Everything felt ethereal. My thoughts were
scattered and confused. People came by and
talked with Mr. Donovan, and came to shake my
hand. Most of them offered their condolences
and a few words. Some put a small gift on the
table. I didn't know why I was getting gifts. I
wasn't sure I wanted to open them.

Slowly, I was starting to feel normal again. I
began to forget my confusion and remembered
my original excitement for the party. I wanted to
dance! The music was calling to me. I made my
way into the crowd. The energy was intense.
Everyone was moving together as if it was
choreographed - no one was out of sync. I had
never experienced anything like it.

The music stopped for a brief moment, and in the sudden silence, a clap of thunder roared through the sky. A percussive *THUMP* drove into the air, thundering through my chest. A massive blinding white light flashed, turning night into day for an instant. The world fell silent, the sky opened, and rain came crashing down. But then, the music came back on, and the party was still alive!

I don't know how long we danced. After a while, the crowd started to thin and spread out. I drifted back towards Mr. Donovan. He was sitting and happily sipping on a large colorful drink.

"How are you doing?" I asked.

He set his drink down and smiled up at me, then laughed and took another sip before answering. "I am fantastic! Thank you!" He went back to his drink. This man consumed alcohol in astonishing quantities.

I noticed the bottle of wine from earlier and picked it up to look at it more closely. The wine inside sloshed around, and I thought I could smell flowers. I set it down and turned back to the crowd of people, still mingling and dancing.

Carl walked up beside me and offered me a bottle of water.

"Thirsty?"

He turned his gaze to the crowd. I could see he had no desire to go onto the dance floor. I cracked open the water and took a long draw. It was ice-cold, crisp and pure, and it revitalized me.

"Thanks! I needed that. Not much for dancing?" I asked, hoping he'd lighten up a little.

"Oh no, I love to dance. Just not with them." He motioned to the dance floor with an absent flick of his hand. "They are not my crowd." He flashed a quick smile. Then, his face seemed to droop a little, and his eyes widened.

I followed his gaze, and my eyes popped open as well.

A woman with raven hair and pale skin approached us from the dance floor. She wore a skin-tight white dress. Her lips were coated in deep red lipstick. She looked at Carl, and her eyes moved slowly from him to me, before settling to meet my gaze. Mr. Donovan sputtered on his drink behind me, but I barely registered the sound of it. She was intimidating. This woman carried herself like she could rule the world if she wanted.

She walked up, leaning uncomfortably close, and smelled me. It was intrusive, and I was a bit taken aback. But, as she pulled away, her scent lingered. I melted. She - her scent - was intoxicating. It was spicy with currant undertones, and it carried an earthy tang to the back of my nose. I unintentionally breathed deep and sighed. I could feel a heat coming from her, and my knees went weak.

"You are Domonic?"

I nodded slowly. I could feel the ring on my finger turn ice cold.

"I was hoping to try your wine," she gestured to the bottle, "but it will need some time to breathe before we drink."

I looked at the bottle and nodded again. I felt the ring start to warm up. I tried to meet her gaze. "Well, if you want to come back to my place, we can get the wine breathing." *What is wrong with me? Smooth Dom, she's going to laugh at you.*

She looked past me at Mr. Donovan for a moment. Her gaze moved to Carl and back to me. Then she took another deep breath through her nose, as if smelling me, moving from my collar bone to my ear. She giggled a familiar giggle.

"Yes, let's go get that wine breathing."

I looked to Carl. He cleared his throat.

"I'll go get the car."

Carl stood up and started heading to the parking lot. The woman smiled, picked up the wine in one hand, and taking my hand in the other. She pulled away from the table with me in tow - not that I was offering any resistance. I could hear Mr. Donovan laughing behind us.

Carl got us to the beach house faster than I imagined. I spent the short ride visualizing how we would be crashing through the door, ripping each other's clothes off. Unfortunately, that's not what happened.

We did rush in the door, but instead of turning to me, she bee-lined to a shelf where she retrieved a decanter for the wine. I stood and watched, dumbfounded, as she ripped the wax and twine free and dumped the wine unceremoniously into the decanter. It glugged and splashed. She seemed to know where everything was. After she poured the wine, she took the cork and brought it to her nose. She braced herself against the bar and rolled the cork in her mouth for a moment before letting out a frustrated sigh and spitting it on the floor. She stood there staring at the wine for an uncomfortable moment, then glanced up at me and chuckled.

"Let's go upstairs and see where you sleep."

I was no longer just aroused - I felt entranced, void of all inhibition... I followed her upstairs obediently, an undercurrent of unexplainable fear prickling my skin.

She looked around the room and nodded appreciatively. I watched her gaze linger on the lockbox. She turned to me, looked me up and down, and then sat on the bed. She flicked off her shoes and settled her gaze in my eyes.

"Rub my feet."

Not what I had expected, but I proceeded to massage her feet. I was no longer sure that this

would lead to anything, but I just felt…
compelled.

"So, how far along are you?" She read the
confusion on my face. "With your inheritance I
mean."

I looked at her and started to feel hazy "I've
only started, I have no idea what to do with
myself."

What happened next is shrouded in fog. I do
clearly remember her fetching the wine and
pouring some in my mouth. She was reciting
some incoherent words. I distinctly recall that I
liked how it tasted. I think we had sex. Or
maybe I watched us have sex… I can't be
certain. It all faded and eventually I slept, and I
dreamt.

~

"So happy to see you again."

I was laying on the ground, surrounded by dead
trees. A faint smell of smoke whispered through
the air. I looked for the source of the voice and
was pleased to see the woman in the white
dress. She was sitting on a small pile of

cushions a few trees away from me. It was like a scene from a nightmare, but I wasn't afraid.

"You probably don't remember much, and I don't blame you for that. I am pleased - you did well. Your uncle picked a suitable heir."

I got up to walk over to her. It took tremendous effort. The smoke had started to thicken and burned my eyes.

"Where are we?" I asked her, "Who are you?" She had never given me her name.

I struggled to move. *Why can't I move?*

She reached behind a pillow and pulled out a small gray rabbit. She laid down, cuddling the rabbit. There was no smoke around her or the pillows.

"If you lay down next to me, I'll tell you."

I tried to move toward her, but my body wouldn't budge. I clenched my fists and focused on my resolve. Something was wrong. My fingers were clenched together, and I realized I couldn't feel my uncle's ring. It wasn't on my hand. I felt a surge of panic and my muscles seized. It was hard to breathe. I tried to focus, to relax, and tried to take a deep breath.

"Move! Move, God damn it!" My voice squeaked out. I tried again, and my legs started to shuffle. I wanted to scream out as I marched forward towards her. When I finally drew in a breath, the smoke burned my lungs and my eyes started to water. It brought me to my knees, so I started to crawl, trying to stay below the smoke. It didn't help.

"Why is there so much smoke?" I choked the words out. My eyes were blurry and watering. I coughed, and spittle flung its way down my chin. I could barely breathe.

She rolled over a little bit, still petting the bunny. "I like the smoke. It keeps people away."

I got close enough to put a hand on one of the pillows. As soon as I did, the smoke eased back and thinned. My eyes stopped aching. My lungs begged for deep breaths. She looked impressed.

"My goodness, you are tenacious."

I pulled myself up and dropped my head on the pillow. She leaned in close and kissed my cheek.

"My name is Freya. This is my home." It was getting easier to breathe now. I didn't move a muscle.

"That's a really nice name. You live in a forest?" She smiled, and her finger caressed my cheek fondly.

"No, the forest is in my home."

I began feeling the dizziness creep in again. My head hurt, and everything started to fade. "What? Wait... I just need a little nap." I muttered.

"Farewell, for now, Domonic" her voice echoed.

The forest faded.

~

I woke up in my bed. The sun was shining. I rolled over and noticed a note on the bedside table. "Until I need you again." A big red lipstick kiss was pressed on the lower part of the page.

"Huh… okay," I grunted. My head was splitting with pain, and I felt dehydrated and hungover. I noticed that the lockbox was upside down. She must have looked it over before she left. "I need water, and a shower."

Laughter drifted up from downstairs. I ignored it and made my way to the bathroom. I showered and scrubbed thoroughly. The hot water felt soothing. I was still sore and fatigued, like a hangover that I couldn't shake. After my shower, I went to get changed and noticed that all the little gift boxes were sitting in a pile at the foot of the bed. I ignored them and went to see what all the laughter was about. When I arrived in the kitchen, I saw only Mr. Donovan sitting down and eating.

"Hey, I brought a lady home last night. Did you see her?"

Mr. Donovan nodded, finished chewing, and sipped some coffee.

"Well lad, she was here, but she left a little bit ago. She said that she was very impressed by your uncle's replacement - well, by you." He was cutting at a pile of eggs as he spoke.

"Well, what does she mean by that?"

Mr. Donovan took a long drink from his coffee and then leaned forward on his elbows.

"Your uncle was a fascinating man. He was just as complicated as he was fascinating though. I never knew another man who had as many lovers as he did - and I'm sure she was one of them." He laughed and went back to his breakfast.

My mouth hung open. It appeared that my uncle had lived a life of wealth and women. I wasn't sure I wanted to inherit that life. Although the idea had a kind of dark appeal, there was really only one woman I really cared about that way, and I wanted more from her than casual sex.

"Well, *I'm* not a complicated man. Is my uncle leaving me a belt with notches in it?"

Mr. Donovan chuckled. I heard a knock at the door. Mr. Donovan got up to answer it. I looked out the window and noticed that the rain had stopped, and the sun was shining. I took a tentative sip of my coffee. Thankfully, there was no whiskey in it this time.

I couldn't make out what was being said at the door, but it sounded like a man's voice. A few minutes later, Mr. Donovan returned and set a large brown box on the table. It clunked and sounded heavy.

"This is addressed to you. It is from… I don't know who."

I looked at the sender's name. It was in a language I didn't recognize. Διόνυσος

"It says it's from Litochoro, Greece!"

I opened the box, and inside there were 12 bottles of aged wine. Each bottle had a twine and wax cap.

"Oh! This must be from the guy at the party last night. I didn't get his name though."

Mr. Donovan nodded along while pouring a liqueur into his coffee.

"Ah, Domonic, I have to go out and take care of a few things. Will you be alright by yourself for a while?"

I grunted as I moved the box of wine. It was far heavier than I expected. "Yeah, I'll just relax for a while. Try to not have sex with anymore strange women, I think."

Mr. Donovan laughed as he walked away.

Later, I wandered around the beach house. I stopped and looked at the lockbox and pondered all the little gifts that had been left for me at the party. I started opening them up. They were all curious little trinkets, oddly shaped wood pieces, and small metal pieces. They all looked like pieces of art, beautifully crafted and as far as I could tell, useless. "I'm inheriting your friends' eclectic art now?" I left them scattered on the floor and got myself cleaned up, planning to take advantage of the nice weather and go for a walk.

When I walked out the front door, I heard none of the city sounds I was used to. It was quite here. There was no traffic, no talking, no noise. Just the roll of the ocean and a faint breeze. The street sign ahead read "Bay Ave." I noticed a bench not far ahead. Feeling refreshed, I sat and rested my arms on the back. It felt like the world just stopped. I fell into the moment of it, my mind was empty, and I felt at peace with everything. It was delightful.

"Is this seat taken?"

The voice startled me. It was raspy, like gravel running down a mountain face. I looked up and saw an older man with a full beard and a fine grey suit standing at the end of the bench. His face had very few wrinkles, though he carried himself with a confidence that only came with age.

"No, help yourself."

He sat down and let out a deep slow sigh. My sense of peace evaporated. Suddenly the moment felt heavy and the air felt dense. He looked over at me;

"You're not ready yet, are you?" It felt more like a statement than a question.

His eyes were a piercing gray. I tried to meet his gaze, but his eyes looked right through me, and I felt like I could hide nothing from him.

"It isn't easy inheriting what you have. Your uncle was a prolific man, in his own way."

Every muscle in my body was rigid. I felt like a cornered rabbit. My heart was pounding in my chest.

"What do you mean? Who are you?" I asked, stuttering the words out with the elegance of a scared child.

"I'm an old acquaintance of your uncle. He called me Zefs. I helped him build his fortune."

I relaxed a little. "Oh, sorry about that Zefs, I didn't recognize you. I don't recall seeing you at the funeral, or the party afterward."

He looked back out over the ocean waters, his eyes dipping from the horizon to the water. There was a faint sound of thunder in the distance.

"It's been a long time since I spoke with him. He was a good man. You will be a good man too, in time." His eyes left the water and he looked back at me. "I sent my son ahead of me. He gave you some wine, I believe. Can you tell me, did you drink it?"

I felt a moment of panic. Maybe the wine was not for drinking. I stammered, "We did, I-I did, yes." But he seemed to relax with the admission.

"Good, that is very good. I hope you enjoyed it. My son has a vineyard that is unmatched; he has a talent for it." He smiled and turned his head back to me. "Best head inside, there is rain coming."

I reached out and shook his hand. "It was nice to meet you Zefs. Tell your son that his wine is out of this world!"

He nodded at me and I started heading back to the beach house.

Zefs was right. The skies opened, and it was pouring by the time I got through the door. I was drenched and cold, and felt ready for a nap. I went up to my room, threw my wet clothes into the shower, dried myself off, and laid down.

Chapter Three
New Beginnings

Ruth sounded happy when I checked in on her and Coaldust.

"Oh no dear, Coaldust is just fine. He has bundles of energy and is just as happy as can be! He even follows me when I go back to my apartment, little sweetie!"

Coaldust never followed me around like that. He'd just lie there and watch me, and meow if he wanted food. I was happy he liked Ruth.

"That sounds nice, Ruth. I might not be home in the next day or two. Can you keep Coaldust for a little while longer?"

Her laugh sounded so nice. It was going to be good seeing her again. It was getting close to her birthday and I knew she had no one else coming to visit her. I should get her something.

"I can keep him here for as long as you like. I like having a little friend around here. He keeps me moving around and it's good for my hip." She chatted on enthusiastically.

I realized that I was now in a position to help her. I knew she had medical bills outstanding from her hip replacement.

"Ruth, I'm going to send you something. Just my way of saying thank you."

Ruth is like family. She always shows up with a container of baked goods on the holidays. If I could adopt her as my Grandmother, I would. She is always willing to help anyone who needs it. I once watched her go out and give a homeless person a knitted blanket because it was a little chilly. She deserves good things in her life, and I was excited to think about what I could do for her.

"Oh Dommy, you don't have to do that, really." That's what you're supposed to say, but I knew she was sincere.

I paused before I put my foot down. "Actually Ruth, I'm going to send you a cheque in the mail. It's going to beat me there, I think. You keep Coaldust company. If you like, I'll see you as soon as I get back."

She sounded wary. "Alright Dommy, you get home safe and we'll see you when you get home."

I was glad to hear Coaldust was being good and everything was calm. Grinning with excitement, I went to my suitcase, and took out my cheque book. This was the first really good thing I was going to do with my newfound wealth. I wrote out a cheque for $50,000. It seemed like the right amount. I had my own money to last the trip, and I wouldn't have to wait long for the rest of the fortune to become available. I spent some time writing her a letter too. I knew Ruth loved getting letters - real letters, not that "easy-mail." I explained everything (well, not everything) I'd experienced in the last couple of days. A little rooting around produced some stamps and an envelope from an odds-and-ends drawer. I stuck the stamp in the corner, wrote out her address, and it was good to go.

That done, my eyes fell on the lockbox.

"How do I get into you?"

I looked it over. Other than the weird holes in the bottom, there was nothing to indicate how to get in. I thought maybe a key would work, but the one Mr. Donovan had didn't turn.

I was startled out of my concentration by the sound of the door flying open.

"Domonic! Are you here?" Mr. Donovan sounded distressed. I ran from my room to the top of the stairs. He was standing in the front doorway, soaking wet, and clutching a black plastic bag.

"Oh good! Here, this is the last thing I am supposed to give you. I had to go back to my office to track it down, but I found it!" He seemed very pleased with himself.

I went down the stairs and took the bag from him. Inside was a big yellow envelope addressed to me. In the envelope were dozens of sheets of paper. Each sheet had a strange geometric shape that was scrawled in the middle of it. Each shape was unique, and every page had a slightly different triangle drawn in the corner. Each one was missing a small segment from the left side, another the right, the third the bottom, and the fourth had a small segment from each side removed. They looked like coloring pages.

"I'm going to get changed, have a drink, then have a nap. What a long drive." He looked exhausted.

I watched him start to take off his clothes as he went upstairs. I went to my room, tossed the envelope in my luggage, and went back downstairs.

Mr. Donovan was pouring himself a drink in the lounge. He was wearing a thick bathrobe.

"Rough day?" I quipped lightly.

"Yes, very rough. I had to drive 4 hours to my office. Then, I ended up in an argument with a few people, which delayed me significantly. It took me a while to find that envelope, and then the drive back here." He downed the entire glass in one shot and started to pour a new one.

"Well, I was going to go find a burger for supper. Did you want me to get you one?"

He didn't seem to hear me.

"Mr. Donovan, did you want a burger for supper?"

He glanced at me and nodded, then went back to pouring.

"All right, I'll be back soon."

It was like a monsoon outside. I sent a text off to summon Carl. A short while later, he pulled up, and I made a run for the car. He didn't have a chance to get out to open the door for me. I hopped in, happy for the shelter from the rain.

"Sir, I have an umbrella. I could have come to the door and walked you to the car."

I looked up at the front of the car. Carl had a large umbrella held up. "Well fuck, I should have thought of that. Anyway, it's a greasy food and beer night. You want to join me and Mr. Donovan?"

The question hung in the air for a moment longer than I expected.

"Sure, I don't have any plans." He started driving without being prompted.

I looked out the window but could not see very far. "Carl, I have a letter I need to mail. Do you know where I can find a mailbox?"

He slowed down and pulled over. "Hand me the letter sir. There is a mailbox on the way."

I handed it over.

I turned my attention to my phone and looked for the nearest drive-thru. I found nothing. "I can't see anything that would indicate a quick bite to eat around here."

Carl had a big smile on his face as he made another turn and came to a stop.

"Sir, if you want a good burger, it takes a little time and some care."

Carl hopped out of the car, ran to a mailbox on the corner, and dropped in the letter. He returned a moment later, and we continued on.

"Your letter has been mailed. Your uncle Michelle and I used to come here for a burger once in a while. This is Kelly's pub. Finn's Pub Burger is the best burger I've ever had."

I looked at the window then back at Carl

"Finn's Pub Burger? Why not Kelly's Pub Burger?"

Carl shrugged with his face as much as his shoulders. We both flung our doors open and made a mad dash from the car to the pub.

I looked at the burgers on the menu, and everything sounded delicious. I couldn't decide - I was hungry and wanted them all.

"Alright Carl, you know what's best. Get three and let's head back to the house."

Carl walked up to the bar, and I got lost in watching the rain through the windows. When I looked up again, Carl was standing beside me with a paper bag in his hand.

"Are you ready to go Mr. Anth?"

I nodded.

When we got back to the beach house, Carl started setting the food out. Mr. Donovan seemed much more at ease.

"So, what is on this burger from heaven Carl?"

Carl looked up at the two of us.

"Flame-cooked chuck burger on a toasted Brioche bun, with crisp lettuce, tomato, onion, and melted Irish cheddar."

It sounded like he was reciting the menu. It also sounded fantastic.

Mr. Donovan perked up and sauntered to the table. "Irish cheddar? Sounds delicious. Let's eat!"

We poured some wine and ate. The burger was as good as Carl had promised. We ate quietly, appreciating the good food, and listened to the rain coming down outside. The only conversation was brief acknowledgement of each other to pour more wine.

When we were done, by silent mutual assent, we went into the lounge and sat down. It was like we were old friends and had hung out like this a hundred times. The rain felt like a blanket pushing the world away. We all put up our feet and relaxed.

I felt waves of catharsis wash through me. I was full, warm, and content and my eyelids were feeling heavy.

"Thanks for this, guys, I really appreciate it."

Mr. Donovan answered with a soft snore.

Carl smiled and waved dismissively "Thank *you,* Mr. Anth. I was worried that you might be a stick in the mud. I'm glad you're not."

I chuckled to myself, closed my eyes, and felt sleep take hold.

~

"I spoke with him. He doesn't know what he has inherited."

I recognized that voice. Why was I hearing a voice?

"Excellent! This is going to be so much fun!"

Her voice sent chills down my spine. I felt like I had heard her voice before too. It felt like nails dragging across a chalkboard. The feeling was awful.

"Perhaps we're going to have to take it easy on this one? Keep him from jumping into the deep end right away..."

That sounded reasonable. The 'deep end' sounded like something I needed to stay as far away from as possible.

"No! You not take away! This is new, is mine, and is for us to have!"

I did not like that voice at all. It sounded like someone was screaming a whisper, with a throat full of liquid.

"Hey, can you all keep it down! I am trying to sleep!" I shouted in my head, thinking it would keep the dream quiet.

"Well, well, well! Looks like you can hear us already. We're expecting great things!" She said.

I jerked awake, rattled. Goosebumps crawled up my entire body. Did I really hear the voice or was it a dream?

Carl and Mr. Donovan were still sleeping in the lounge. It had grown dark outside, but at least the rain had died down. My heart and head were heavy, and a pensive state settled around me. I didn't know what to make of all of this. I made my way up to my room and laid down in bed. Flashes of lightning lit the room through the curtains, and wild cracks of thunder echoed from deep in the storm. I needed to sleep, and I fell back into it with ease.

Ring ring!
Ring ring!

I instinctively reached over and grabbed for my phone. I could still hear the rain falling gently. "Rain, unending rain," I muttered as I felt around on the nightstand. I finally managed to find my phone and answered it groggily.

"Hello?"

"Fucking guy! Y-you think you're something hot shit, hey buddy? J-j-just up and quitting like a f-fucking fuck!"

The words were shouted and stuttered. I was stunned - I hadn't expected a drunk Kyle on the line.

"Kyle? What are you doing? It's gotta be three in the-"

"FUCK YOU! I fucking hate you so much! Traitor-dog-whore-nut-fuck! You shit-eater you cuz you ARE what you EAT! Hahahahahaha-

The line went quiet.

"Kyle...?"

Nothing, no response. I looked at my phone and hung up. I felt the shock of his words. One of my closest friends felt betrayed, and I couldn't explain myself to him. I felt the clench of guilt in my stomach. I wanted to throw up, to purge the tight nausea in my gut.

"Maybe a big ass cheque will make him feel better." I felt dirty even saying it, and immediately regretted it. Kyle wasn't the kind of person who you could just pay off to make him feel better. He was allowed to hate me - I would probably hate me - and I had no right to try and take that away from him.

I was still exhausted but too rattled to go back to sleep, so I spent the next hour or so mindlessly surfing the internet. I eventually fell asleep with my phone still in my hand.

~

Ding!

Di-Ding!

I woke to the sound of my phone dinging notifications at me. "Hmm?" I felt around for my phone, which was now tangled in the sheets. Finding it, I looked at what was coming in. The bank was notifying me of transfers into various accounts. The money was there. A *lot* of money.

I stared at it in silence as a huge smile crept onto my face. I thought to myself.

"I guess it's time to start making some changes to my life. I'll have to get insurance, sort out a will, and celebrate with something stupid. Maybe I'll upgrade my ticket home to first class."

I had no clue what to do. I could do anything I wanted now.

I grabbed my laptop and went downstairs, where I found Mr. Donovan still fast asleep in his chair. Carl had apparently left. I settled in at the bar and started looking up real estate options in Seattle. The prices were a little shocking. I found myself having to constantly remind myself of my change in financial situation. I looked at pre-furnished lofts, bungalows, high rise condominiums, and tremendous houses that I couldn't reasonably think of any way to fill. All of them were cheap compared to what I had access to now. I wondered what kind of house Nicole would like?

"House, condo, apartment, bungalow? I guess I'll have to check some of these places out when I get back."

The rain had finally stopped, and I was grateful for the break from it. Mr. Donovan stirred. I could tell he was starting to wake up, so I made my way into the kitchen to put on some coffee. He stumbled in a few minutes later.

"Good morning, coffee brewing? Good, excellent. I might need something for the pain." He motioned toward his head.

I went over to the cupboards and found an assortment of painkillers, including Midol. I grabbed two of those for him then poured some coffee.

"Here you go: coffee - black and strong, pain medication. Be healed, my friend." I waved my arms with a flourish.

He chuckled and groaned then appreciatively took the coffee and pills.

"Mmmm, thank you, my boy. I am going to lay down until this all kicks in." He shuffled off with his coffee.

I made myself some toast and sat down at the kitchen table, still pondering. After breakfast, I went back up to my room. I picked up the lockbox again and looked it over. I couldn't figure out how to get into this thing. The many holes in the bottom didn't help either. There was no pattern or design that I could see.

"I like puzzles, but I can't…"

I stopped and looked at the tiny art pieces I had been given. Each piece was an odd sort of geometric shape with strange gouges and ridges scattered randomly across their surfaces. Everything else thus far had been weird enough. I reached over and grabbed one of them. I examined it and held it up against the bottom of the box. I thought there might be a spot for it. It was the correct width, and I was able to slide it in smoothly, although it didn't do anything.

"This is either going to be really interesting, or really frustrating."

I spent a few hours trying different pieces all around the bottom of the lockbox. I had no success in making anything fit or click in any meaningful way. I tossed all the pieces on the bed and the lockbox next to it.

"I have no idea what to do with you." I ran my hands through my hair and sighed. "Lunch now, puzzle later."

I walked down to Kelly's. There was a slight chill in the air, but at least it wasn't raining. The path to Kelly's was peaceful. A few people out walking their dogs waved at me, and I waved back. I could hear other homes entertaining guests. Faint music played, laughter and the sounds of dishes clattered against the din of their revelry.

When I entered the pub, it was quiet, and nobody was behind the bar. I couldn't see anyone around.

"Hello? Anyone here?"

No answer.

I walked a little further into the pub and around a corner. Three women were sitting at a table. They all had sunglasses on, which was odd not only because they were indoors but because it was still dark and cloudy outside. One of the women was quite old and drinking wine, another was middle-aged and stuffing her face with toast points. The third was younger, attractive, and slowly sipping away at a drink. They were all sitting on the far side of the table, looked up at me, and passed whispers between them. It caught me off guard. Was I paranoid, or were they talking about me?

I walked up to the bar and sat down, figuring someone would be along shortly. I was wrong. I waited a couple of minutes and looked around for a bell to ring.

"No one is coming right now. They have a delivery in the back that isn't going quite right." Her voice quivered a bit like she was holding back a giggle.

I looked over, and the oldest of the three waved her hand at me. I smiled and waved back, then reached for a menu, trying to dismiss the awkward conversation.

I jumped when I felt a hand on my shoulder. I hadn't heard her come up behind me.

"Are you eating, or are you drinking?"

Her voice had a southern ring to it, and it poured into my ears like honey. I looked at her dreamily. She had tousles of brilliant blonde hair falling around her shoulders. She smiled and watched my eyes stray up and down her face, hair, chest, and down to her hips. She looked to be about my age. I unintentionally smiled and tried to focus.

"I was ummm... planning on food, but a drink doesn't sound bad either."

She walked behind the bar and pulled up a glass for me, then took her time looking over the bottles. I heard her make some discerning "hmms" and "ahhs" while she looked around. Eventually, she made some selections and brought over four bottles of what I correctly assumed to be whiskeys.

"I remember when I first got here, I thought this place was a dump. I couldn't figure out why the others liked it so much."

She carefully measured out equal parts from each bottle into a glass and stirred.

"After a little while, I figured it out. It's the people! I guess we won't be around much longer though, with the funeral being over and all."

She put some crushed ice in a glass and poured the blended drink over top.

"Oh well, it has been a treat being here. I've seen some family that I haven't seen in a long time."

She covered the glass, strained the liquor into a shot glass, and slid it over to me. I drank it down. It was smooth and delicious, with a slight chill.

"Thank you, that was fantastic. What's it called?"

She smiled and put the bottles away. "The Four Horsemen. I'm glad you liked it."

We were interrupted by a sound from the door.

"Sister, it is time to be going." The other two ladies were standing there, apparently ready to leave. She pouted her lips and waved goodbye. I watched her go - it was hard not to.

"Do you need a menu?" I looked back to the bar. An older man was looking at me, holding out a thin sheet of paper.

"Yeah, yeah, sorry about that." I scrolled down the list, and my eyes landed on a chowder that looked pretty good. "Can I get a bowl of chowder?"

He nodded and went back into the kitchen, bringing out a bowl of soup in less than a minute. The first spoonful was sharp and buttery. Chunks of potato, seasoned with a harmonious combination of bay leaf, lemon, onion, and pepper melted in my mouth. Every time I brought the spoon to my mouth, I felt some of the anxiety and stress in my shoulders melt away. I closed my eyes and savored it, hints of fish broth crawling deep into my taste buds. I enjoyed every spoonful and was delighted when I discovered some perfectly cooked clams nestled near the bottom of the bowl.

I looked up from my soup to discover that the rain had started trickling down again.

"The sunshine was nice while it lasted." I observed, breaking the silence

The man at the bar grunted. He didn't seem interested in conversation, and he turned and walked into the back. I hurriedly finished the last of my chowder and tossed $10.00 on the bar.

"Money's on the bar, I've gotta go." I called toward the kitchen. I wanted to get back to the beach house before the rain got worse.

When I returned, I found Mr. Donovan working over a pile of papers and Carl sleeping in a recliner. I climbed the stairs to my room, took off my wet clothes, and laid down on the bed. I just wanted to relax. My eyes felt heavy enough to close on their own.

I woke up about a little while later to the sound of heavy rain, my head pounding with pain. I stared out the window and pondered. I knew it was getting close to the time I would need to get back home. I missed Coaldust, and I figured I had to speak with Kyle in person.

There was a faint knock at my door.

"Mr. Anth, are you awake?"

I sat up, and my head throbbed.

"Yeah Carl, come in."

He opened the door and looked around tentatively, as if he was expecting someone else to be in the room.

"Sir, I just wanted to know if you would like me to drive you back to Seattle, or if you would like me to meet you there."

I had forgotten about Carl, and hadn't thought about him coming back with me. I still wasn't used to the idea of him being a part of my life.

"I don't know, Carl. You probably have things to do. I'm going to fly back to Seattle to take care of a few things, and then I don't know what I'll do."

Carl nodded. "As you wish sir. Here is my card. If you visit the site on the back, it will install an app on your phone that will let you see where the car is at any time. You can even message or call me directly through the app."

I raised an eyebrow. I hadn't pegged Carl as a tech-savvy person. "Thanks, Carl!" He turned to leave, and I got up to close the door behind him.

He waved over his shoulder. I opened my luggage and took out a small pill case. My head was still pounding for some reason.

"Over the lips and past the gums…" I muttered before swallowing two painkillers. I laid back down to wait for my head to stop hurting, and eventually fell asleep. Tomorrow was my return home and the start of a new beginning.

Chapter Four

Designer Life

"Alright sir, I have upgraded your ticket to first class. Was there anything else I could help you with?"

I had no idea what else you could ask for, so I asked.

"I don't know, I've never done this before, what else can you help me with?"

She paused - clearly the question was unexpected. I could hear the clacking of the keyboard for several long moments before she returned to the phone.

"I'm sorry sir, I don't have anything additional that I could offer you for a domestic flight. If you ever travel internationally though, please do request the Executive Suites package."

I liked the sound of that. "I will! Thank you for your help."

I hung up and started packing my bags. I looked around at the lockbox and the little gifts I had been given. With a deep sigh, I headed down to see Mr. Donovan.

"Hey, I'm just getting ready to go. I wanted to ask you, that lockbox and the other things, can I leave them here until I'm done in Seattle?"

Mr. Donovan nodded and looked up from his paperwork.

"I can forward it all to you if you like. I wouldn't advise leaving those things here unguarded though. I don't plan on living here all the time. Speaking of which, is Seattle where you plan on staying for the most part?"

I hadn't invested very much thought in it yet. Too much had been happening.

"I don't know yet. I could stay in Seattle, or move back to Ontario even. Or I could just float around. I don't know... I guess I was planning on sorting out some things once I was done here and back home in Seattle, and then figuring out where to settle." I thought for a second, "And yes, regarding the box and gifts, it can all be forwarded."

Mr. Donovan turned and grabbed his coffee. He took a long sip before he spoke.

"Very good. I told Carl I won't be needing his help. I told him to get ready to go to Seattle. And of course, you will want the car. It does belong to you after all. When Carl drops you off, he will begin his drive to Seattle." He turned and set his coffee down, looking me up and down. "I will be out there at the end of the month to check on you." He walked over to his briefcase, opened it up, and pulled out a pocket book. "This is for you. It is a contact book, and these are all of my possible contact numbers - everything from my mobile to my brother's house. Keep calling through these numbers if you need me."

I was shocked at how available Mr. Donovan was making himself.

"I appreciate it. Can you tell me if there is a closer airport than Baltimore that I can fly back to Seattle out of?"

Mr. Donovan thoughtfully stroked his chin for a moment.

"Norfolk. You can fly out of there, certainly, it's much closer as well."

I clapped my hands together then reached out and shook his hand.

"Great! I just finished upgrading to first class. A transfer should be easy enough! Thank you for everything Eric. I'll see you in a week or so."

He nodded and waved as he returned to his work.

When I finished packing, I called Norfolk International and got my flight transferred from Baltimore to Norfolk. I texted Carl too and told him I was ready to go whenever he was free. I knew it was only a couple of hours to my layover in Norfolk, and then I would have a lot of time to waste there. I liked that idea. No rush, no need to worry about getting anywhere fast. I bundled up the lockbox, the manila folder, the little gifts, and the wine to get them ready for mailing.

Ding, dong!

I went down the stairs and welcomed Carl in. He wasn't wearing a suit this time. Rather, he was in shorts and a hoodie with flip-flops.

"Hey, Domonic!"

He didn't call me Mr. Anth, that was nice.

"Carl, looking casual." I nodded at him.

I went upstairs to start bringing things down. Carl went off to speak with Mr. Donovan. I started by taking down my luggage. When I reached the bottom of the stairs, Carl came around the corner.

"Hey, I'll take that to the car, and be right back to grab whatever else you want me to bring to Seattle."

It took us a couple of trips, but we got it all packed tidily. We had a quick farewell drink with Mr. Donovan, said our goodbyes, and then we were off. I sat up front with Carl this time.

"You're wondering why I'm not in a suit?"

I nodded.

"This is my day off. I'm going to be heading to Seattle after I drop you at the airport."

"Right on. Well, my flight won't be leaving until 10:00 pm. Did you want to do anything in Norfolk before we head our separate ways?"

I had no idea what we could do in Norfolk, but I thought Carl might.

Carl looked at me with some apprehension. "You mean spend time together in public?"

"Yeah, well, I didn't mean you should suit up and wait in the car... I mean, I'm not Miss Daisy." I wanted to work on developing a friendship with Carl.

He laughed a soulful, genuine laugh before he replied. "I guess we could get some food or see a movie." He smiled as I nodded my agreement.

"Great!" We both exclaimed, laughing in unison.

The drive to Norfolk was pleasant. We seemed to be leaving the rain behind us. When we entered Norfolk, I had no clue what to do or where to go to waste some time.

As I looked out the window for inspiration, everything seemed to go quiet. I felt dizzy. My vision was swimming and churning, a deep, loud sound rang through my ears -*whoosh, whoosh, whoosh.* I couldn't keep my thoughts straight. I looked toward Carl, but he kept driving, apparently unaware of my discomfort. I closed my eyes, but that made the vertigo worse. Feeling like I was spinning, I turned back to my own window in time to see the passenger side of the car start to crumple inward.

Everything moved in slow motion. I watched with interest as the front end of a truck started pushing into the car and a large white pillow exploded toward me on the inside of the door, slammed into my face. The plastic headlight cover of the truck cracked as it forced itself into my door. My reflection in the side view mirror shattered into multiple images, then each image flew away. There was no fear. Rather, I felt my mind disconnect from my body, and I watched from outside myself as my body whipped to the side. The sound crashed down around me as the collision jerked my senses back to reality. I could hear the crunch of the impact, the gunshot sound of the airbag, and the scraping of metal and plastic. The car flipped up on its side, rolling violently and flinging my head back into the door. Decanters of liquor whirled around the inside like dice in a cup. The last thing I saw was one of them flying at my face.

They never tell you how immediate it is, being knocked out. Just a sudden "POP" and you're out. You don't know you're unconscious. And your conscious mind is just scrambling, trying to do damage control while it lets the lizard part of your mind handle the coin-flip on whether you're going to piss yourself or start spasming.

~

"He has a head injury - something struck him right here. He's breathing and has a steady pulse. How's the black fella?"

I tried to turn my head to see Carl. My head wasn't doing what I wanted it to do though.

"He looks pretty bad. The ambulance will get him. Hurry up, let's get this guy packed up. The boss won't want to wait."

Someone was standing over me. From the corner of my eye, I was pretty sure he had a beard, and thin hair topped his head with gray creeping in. The other guy was young with short black hair and was clean shaven.

My vision was swimming, and my body was cooperating with them more than it was with me. They moved me easily and lifted me into their trunk. I couldn't resist. I was panicked, but somehow, despite myself, I drifted into sleep.

I don't know how long it was before I woke up. I heard shouting, though the words were lost to me, muffled by the well-insulated trunk I was in. Thankfully, my body was starting to respond, moving to my commands again. I kicked my foot out against where I thought the tail light might be. My knees felt like they were heavily bruised, and the effort hurt. After a few solid thumps, I heard a crack, and some new light gleamed in. I wormed around until I could see outside. I grunted involuntarily. My limbs and body felt like I had been beaten. The two men who had taken me were standing back-to-back with pistols pointed at the darkness. They looked terrified. Back-to-back, they slowly rotated in circles, and their arms shook with fear.

"Come out and fight!" The younger one shouted.

I could see the older of the two scanning the edge of the darkness.

"Will you shut up!" he growled at his partner before addressing the darkness. "Hey! Listen to me - we're not going to hurt him. We're taking him to our boss, a-a friend of yours. I promise!"

As the words left his mouth, I felt the vehicle jolt. Their eyes looked up slightly. Their hands dropped by their sides, and their guns slipped from their hands. A soft, radiant light bathed them. They gasped in unison, then slowly their expressions changed into elated smiles, their eyes rolling back in their heads. The sound of rushing air tore through the clearing, and everything was covered in a maelstrom of dust and blinding white light. The grass on the side of the road blew flat, and in an instant, it was quiet again. The air stilled. When the dust finally settled and the light faded, the men were gone.

Oh God, what the fuck is happening!?

I panicked and started scratching at the trunk lid. I wanted to get out! I wanted to run! The adrenaline coursed through my veins and I was shredding the cloth covering of the trunk, my nails breaking from the effort. I was relieved when my finger felt a cable tug, and then the trunk lid popped free.

YES! Time to get the fuck outta here!

I threw the trunk lid up and rolled out, falling hard on the ground. The sudden painful reminder of my battered state brought tears to my eyes. The two pistols were on the ground, in front of my face. My abductors appeared to be gone. I was on a dirt road in the middle of nowhere. But at least the vehicle seemed intact. I slowly and carefully got to my feet.

"What the fuck is going on?" I called aloud.

The moon was full and bright, but I couldn't see anything or anyone else around. The car engine was still running. I went around to the driver side door and peered inside. There was no one else there. I opened the door and found a bag with my keys, phone, and wallet inside. I quickly grabbed up my phone and started dialing 9-1-1.

"No need to call anyone."

The voice came from behind me. It was powerful and confident, mind-bendingly familiar, and carried a chill up my spine. I knew his voice.

"I have taken care of them - you are safe now." The tone in the voice shifted and changed from confident to concerned as he spoke.

I felt a wave of relief, I turned around slowly and saw a familiar face. The man from the wake, the one had given me the extremely old wine bottle, was standing there smiling at me.

"You, you're... from the wake... for my uncle."

He nodded. He looked at the car inquisitively before looking back to me. He stepped forward, his hand extended to shake mine. I hesitated, but his smile seemed genuine. The warmth of it was almost tangible, and it seemed to warm the chill air around us.

"Thank you for helping me. Where did they go? And what was that bright light? Where's your vehicle?"

He smiled again, hushing my questions by silently pulling me into an embrace. He smelled of figs mashed into autumn leaves.

"All in good time, my friend. I think it's time we got to know one another."

Suddenly he was gone. I stumbled and fell. I was on my back looking up at the night sky. I couldn't see properly - everything looked as though I was observing it through tunnel vision. My hearing was off too - sounds stretched and blended together into a muffled confusion. And then my body moved, not from my will but all on its own! My body stood easily. The pain from the accident was gone, and my nails were no longer hurting. My arms moved on their own, and my hands came up in front of my face. I could see the broken nails mending right in front of me. All signs of my injuries were suddenly non-existent. I watched as my body casually walked over to the car, got in, buckled the seatbelt, and drove down the road.

"Stay calm, Mr. Anth. I'll be relatively gentle with you."

I could hear him clearly as his thought rang around me. It was soft, confident, and reassuring.

I couldn't even focus enough to respond to him. His voice echoed through my mind.

"If ever there was a good time to be had, we shall have it."

I managed to stutter "What... what is happening?!" At least I think I said it out loud - I couldn't hear myself. Maybe I just thought it. All I could feel was myself smiling his smile. I felt paralyzed, I had no control over myself.

"Your proprioception may be confused for a short time my friend, stay calm. We will synchronize soon."

I watched myself drive down the road. Eventually, city lights came into the distance. I drifted in and out of what was happening. I managed to get a reliable hold on my vision and hearing, but it took a lot of focus and energy. I refocused as we (I?) parked in front of a casino. He (I?) grabbed my wallet, stepped out of the vehicle and walked in. We headed straight up to the chip cage.

"I need five thousand in large chips." It was my voice, but it didn't sound like me.

The cage operator nodded and started filling out a form.

"Do you have an account with us, sir?" She looked up and smiled at me in a way that women don't normally smile at me. She looked younger than me, with brown hair and blonde highlights. She looked me up and down. If it were me in charge of my body, my heart would have started racing. I kind of liked it. With him in charge though, my body was cool and collected.

"No. I would like to start one though."

She slid a form to us through the slot at the bottom of the cage window and he started filling it out. He handed it back with my ID and both of my credit cards. She looked up at me, then picked up the phone and dialed. I felt terribly anxious, but there was no feeling of nervous sweat on my brow.

"Mr. Anth, I guarantee you will not lose any money tonight."

The clerk hung up her phone and slid over a chip tray with an assortment of chips. "Here you are sir. If you need anything at all, please don't hesitate to ask."

He leaned his elbow on the edge of the counter and smiled at her. "I'll be around for a little while. If you need anything at all, don't hesitate to find me." He winked.

She blushed furiously. He held her gaze for a moment longer before walking away.

Wow, she is smitten with you. I thought to the person in control of my body. He just smiled and kept walking.

We approached a roulette table. He gestured to the dealer and asked for five thousand on 22 black. The dealer motioned at a small sign indicating a maximum of $120.

I took a moment to gather my thoughts and. *Thank God, that's a lot of money to throw away on roulette.*

I felt my face smile again and watched as my hand motioned to the pit boss. He came over, looking at me like someone had ruined his day.

"I want to put five thousand on 22 black, no limit payout."

The pit boss held up a finger indicating that he needed a moment. He stepped away and spoke into a radio. Our roulette dealer had a smug look on his face.

"Thank you, Mr. Anth, by all means."

Both the dealer and I were shocked, although his look of surprise was mixed with anger. The man in charge of my body wasn't fazed.

"James, Mr. Anth is authorized for one no-limit wager on any number he would like on this table. After that, the table maximums are in place again."

The pit boss tapped his knuckles on the side of the table and motioned for us to place a wager. I watched the five thousand in chips slide on the table, as my hands pushed it into place.

"22 black" I heard myself say.

The exchange had gathered some interest from the other players at the table. A beautiful woman moved to a seat beside us. She had vibrant red hair and pale skin. She slid a chip in with our pile.

"What the heck, one hundred on 22 black!" She looked at us and smiled prettily.

"I hope this pays out, that's my last chip!" She exclaimed, then chuckled and patted my hand. "I'm just giving you the gears, handsome."

My head turned to her and smiled a warm, confident smile. Other chips were placed as the ball went into the track.

"No more bets" the dealer called out.

Everyone else had their eyes glued to the ball, but my eyes were caught by shoulder-length red hair bobbing up and down. She had stunning green eyes, which were following the ball along with everyone else's. She was chewing on a straw that she had plucked from her drink absent-mindedly. I could feel the man driving my body sigh and look back to the ball in the track. It had started to bounce around. I didn't like the idea of losing this much money gambling.

Mr. Anth, calm down, please, your anxiety is very tiring. Enjoy the ride.

A moment later everything erupted.

"22 Black!" the dealer and the redhead both cried out at the same time.

The pit boss looked stunned as everyone at the table cheered and started patting us on the back. A woman around my age came up with a drink tray and asked for our orders. She looked like she was more interested in my – his - our winnings. Her eyes were predatory as she looked us up and down, waiting for a response.

"Wine, for everyone in your establishment," he announced. "Make an announcement that wine is on the house until the sun rises."

Her blonde hair waved as she shook her head, waiting for a punchline. Our blank stare made it clear that he was not kidding. When she finally realized he wasn't, she turned and walked away.

Our chips were loaded into trays in front of us. $175,000. I watched as my hand reached out and sent a brown $5,000 chip towards the dealer, and he quickly slid it into his tip slot.

"Thank you, Mr. Anth!"

Our eyes looked around the table, and we slid each of the people here a brown chip. Everyone at the table had their mouths hanging open. Our chips had dwindled down to $135,000. We simply turned and walked away to the chip cage.

"Cash ten thousand, and this is for you, and one for you." He slid both of the cage workers a $5,000 chip.

They excitedly waved their tips to the camera up above and produced ten thousand in cash.

"Thank you, ladies."

We turned to walk away from the cage with the remainder of the chips. An unimposing man with thin hair and a slim build stood in our way.

"Mr. Anth, I am Balthazar. I hope your evening is going well. We would like to provide you with complimentary use of our penthouse suite."

I could feel that smile on my face again, and I was starting to like it.

"Yes, my evening is going well, and I will need use of that suite, certainly."

We hefted the chips in my hands. "Now, Balthazar, if you'll please excuse me, I have to go find the woman who took my wine order."

Balthazar coughed and raised his hand to stop us from moving forward.

"We did receive a ludicrous wine order; I wanted to confirm that with you. You want everyone here to have unrestricted access to wine until the sun rises?" His face looked painfully hopeful that this was not actually the case.

"I absolutely do. Anyone who asks for wine tonight should receive it free of charge, regardless of the cost. Thank you for confirming that, although I would still like the announcement to occur overhead."

Balthazar closed his eyes and nodded. We stepped around him and walked away without saying another word.

We returned to the roulette table and played table maximums for a few more spins, winning every time. Most of the winnings we passed around to other patrons and the dealer. Shortly after, the announcement was made.

"Ladies and gentlemen, at the generosity of Mr. Anth, all wine is on the house tonight until the sun rises. Please feel free to place an order with any of the serving staff on the floor or at the bars."

Everyone at the table smiled and looked at us. They seemed enchanted by us – me - him. I had never felt anything like this. It was intoxicating.

We left roulette and headed toward the craps tables. There was a sizeable crowd of people following us, including the gorgeous redhead from the roulette table. We walked up to the craps table, and my eyes carefully looked over every inch of it. I wondered what he was looking for. After several moments, he took our chips and set them down, sliding them over to a placement that read "All or nothing at all

176:1". The crowd stood, staring at the stupidity.

We looked at the dealer.

"There is no limit on this table, or you have no sign that there is a limit. So, I would like to wager $115,000 - all or nothing."

Three pit bosses were walking over to the table. One of them went up to the dealer and bent down. He picked up a maximum bet sign.

"You dropped this, don't let it fall again."

The table limit was $1,000. We looked around and he counted everyone in the crowd. There were 16 people surrounding us.

"Who wants $1,000 to bet with us? You keep your winnings!" he asked.

Everyone around us cheered, took their chips from us, and placed their bets. The pit bosses looked worried. He took the dice and threw them. 12, 2, 11, 10, 9, 4, 8, 5, and finally, 6. There was a split second of silence, then everyone screamed in excitement. Each of us had just won $176,000

The blur of the moment, the heady intoxication of winning, the… hand on my groin? The redhead was literally grabbing my attention. We smiled and walked towards the elevators. Along the way, I watched my hands beckon the serving girl who took our drink orders to join us. My hand pointed at the woman from the chip cage. She came with us as well.

We entered the suite. The women were all pulling at my body, trying to undress me. Someone started music playing. Beside the bed were a half dozen bottles of wine. Everyone fell into a rhythm. Their hands worked at my clothes and each other's. Fingers and nails pulled at me, dragging me onto the bed, lips kissed at my neck and chest. One of them took me into their mouth, and we moaned at the delight. I felt fine hairs tickle my nose before he committed to pleasing whoever was now straddling my head. My hands absently caressed the sides of this woman, and then I was plunged into ecstasy, tendrils of energy pulsing from my body into the warmth of these women. Their pleasure was tangible. I could feel it as they felt it, deep inside me. I knew exactly what to do, what angle and motion they craved, and I obliged, feeling the increased intensity within myself as well. Our bodies worked in unison. As I positioned the serving girl in front of me, she buried her face between the thighs of the cage worker lying on the bed. The redhead from the roulette table was nested above her face. She caressed and kissed the cage worker's breasts, locking eyes with us and gasping. I could feel all three of them, and myself. The pleasure was moving as one through all of us, and my body swayed back and forth. Every thrust sent a ripple of energy through all three women. I felt the combined sensation of giver and receiver. A heat grew behind my belly button. As it grew the redhead put her hands on her abdomen. Her face contorted and all three women moaned loudly. Their bodies seized and tensed. Their hands grasped against sheets and each other's bodies. My body erupted with heat. It moved through the women and the room, the endorphins pulsing through my veins like an incredible high.

The women gave in to exhaustion, collapsing on the bed. I relaxed amongst them for a few moments, then felt my body stand up and walk to the window. The windows fogged as the sun crested over the horizon and bathed the room in light.

He spoke out loud to me.

"Thank you, Domonic. I hope I was gentle enough for you."

I regained control of my body and immediately felt incredible fatigue sweep through me. I stumbled to the bed and collapsed beside the pile of women.

I woke up in a panic. I looked around at the bed and the suite. It was just me - I was in control of my own body. The ladies must have left at some point. The only indication they had ever been in the room was the memories I had of the night before.

I collapsed on the bed, shaking and terrified.

"What's happening to me?"

I felt sick. I got up and went to the washroom. I felt cold and clammy, and made it to the toilet just in time to throw up. I felt like I needed a shower. I stood up and was torn between more sleep or washing away the sticky feeling of the night before. I chose sleep. I stumbled back out to the bed and wrapped myself in blankets. I needed to feel normal again. I closed my eyes.

pop

A notification on my phone woke me. I looked at the screen to find appointment reminders. There was a tailor coming to my room, I had a meeting with the owner of the casino, and I had a massage scheduled. Before I could read more, there was a soft knock at the suite door.

knock knock knock

"Mr. Anth, it is Gerald. You emailed me to come fit you for some suits."

"Uhh yeah, come in…"

The voice was muffled on the other side of the door. "Sir, the door is locked. I can't come in." I got up, wrapped myself in a blanket, and opened the door for him.

Gerald entered the suite, pulling a large wardrobe closet on wheels.

"Ah, good morning sir. If you need to do anything before we begin, please do so now. I shall prepare my things."

He had a tight smile and a pencil-thin mustache, a very professional look.

"Yeah, I need to shower. Be out right away!"

I shuffled into the bathroom. The shower felt amazing. There were three shower heads spraying me. It was almost like a baptism, leaving me reborn from last night's events.

I came out to a handful of housekeeping staff working fervently to clean and organize the room. Gerald was sitting and having a coffee.

"Excellent, Mr. Anth. Please, right up here."

He stood me in front of a mirror and took my measurements. He did not talk much, just measured me and marked notes down in a fine red leather book. I endured his efforts. I was tired of being touched by other people. My fatigue was palpable. His touch was deft and gentle, as if he was afraid to break me.

He pulled out cloth samples and held them up against me, asking what I liked best.

"You're the master here. I guess you be the artist, and I'll be the canvas."

Gerald's eyes lit up with a fire that I hadn't expected. He fervently pulled out different cloth bolts, pinning and marking like a madman. I stood as still as a statue. When he was done, he went to the other side of his wardrobe closet on wheels. I heard some clattering and went around to look. I watched him set up a sewing machine.

He laid out the fabric, measured and cut out pieces, then started pinning and sewing the suit together, right there in the room.

I put my clothes from yesterday back on. They smelled awful, but they were all I had. I was famished. I went downstairs and was greeted by the smell of a breakfast buffet. The wait staff greeted me by name as I entered the restaurant. The tills were closed and covered. The offerings in the warm trays were breakfast sausages, hash browns, scrambled eggs, toast, pancakes, and I also found a waffle station. I took a bit of everything that was readily available, not stopping to make a waffle. I managed to pour some orange juice too. There were other guests at breakfast as well, although none that I recognized. Some of them recognized me though. They raised glasses of mimosas. I raised my juice back to them. I went back to my room with the food.

I went back to the room to find Gerald almost done the first suit. I sat the food down and then called the front desk.

"Mr. Anth, how can I help you?"

Somehow the voice on the phone reminded me of the crash. I realized I needed to get back and make sure Carl was okay.

I abandoned my breakfast. My hunger was gone. "I need some clean clothes and a car rental." I spoke firmly.

She paused. I could hear her keyboard clicking away.

"Mr. Anth, I see you have a vehicle in the parking spot for the suite already, and I will have someone come up with a selection of clothes for you."

I had forgotten about the car we drove here with.

"Uh, thanks."

Soon after, the concierge was at my door, and I was looking at a selection of underwear and clothing. I picked out an assortment of clothing and my sizes were returned to the room in short order. Gerald was done with his suit too.

"Mr. Anth, here you are!"

The suit was slate gray and looked fantastic!

"Thanks, Gerald, this looks really nice. Let me help you pack up."

"Um. Mr. Anth, don't you want to try it on?" He seemed confused.

"No, I have to rush. You measured, and if it doesn't fit, I'll just run it to another tailor. I have to go!"

I got him out the door with all his tailoring equipment. He tried to thank me as I closed the door.

I got changed and ready to leave. I had no luggage, just my suit, and dirty clothes. I stuffed the dirty laundry in the bottom of the suit bag. I went down to the front desk to check out and was greeted by Balthazar.

"Mr. Anth, leaving us already?"

I nodded "Yes, I have things I need to do. Just going to check out and be on my way."

He looked at the front desk clerk and motioned for their attention. He spoke with a hopeful tone.

"Mr. Anth, would you like to maintain your room here?"

I shook my head. "No, I should be good. Just need to check out." My fingers tapped impatiently on the countertop.

He sighed and went behind the front desk, processed some paperwork, and handed me a check-out sheet. It showed a balance owing to me $217,214.46 and listed expenses for a significant amount of wine, clothes, and the tailor.

I signed it and gave it back to him. He looked up at me.

"Do you want your remaining balance in cash or cheque, sir?"

I thought about it briefly and shrugged at him. "Whatever is faster. I need to go, now."

He turned pale as the words left my mouth, swallowing hard before calling it into the cage. Balthazar handed me my vehicle keys and then walked away. I was greeted a few minutes later by two security guards who handed over a large heavy suitcase.

"It's all in here."

I thanked them and went to the parking lot. I found the boat we arrived in, rust spots ruined the dirty beige color of the side panels, but I had no other way to get back. In fact, I realized I had no idea where I had to get back to.

"Shit, where is that card?" I checked my pockets and looked through the car. I finally found it on the floor in the back seat. "Yes!" I quickly typed in the URL on the back of the card, and as promised, I was prompted to install an application. I could see my own car on the map, at an impound lot. I clicked the button to call Carl.

ring ring, ring ring, ring ring

"Norfolk General, this is Dr. Bailey."

I took a deep breath. My blood felt like it had turned to ice. My thoughts immediately went to terrible places, and I imagined him unresponsive in a hospital bed with tubes running into his arms and mouth. My heart was pounding in my chest.

"Hi, I'm looking for Carl, we were in an accident together. I'm calling his phone… -" I could hear some muffled overhead pages being made and my anxiety was going crazy.

"Mr. Salem? Yes, he was brought in by ambulance yesterday, can I ask who you are sir?"

"I'm his employer, Domonic. I just want to know if he's okay." Her voice softened a little

"He should be fine. Carl is sleeping right now. If you want to see him just go to information and ask for his room number. He should have a bed pretty soon."

"Thank you, I will be there as soon as I can." I hung up and got in the car. I knew where to go now.

Norfolk General was only about an hour away. The reality of what had taken place was slowly setting in; the shock of being possessed, the chaos from the abduction and to the night of revelry I was forced to endure… to enjoy? It felt unreal. I couldn't afford to focus on it right then, or I would get lost in the thoughts, and I needed to see Carl. I felt more alone and guiltier than ever before in my life.

Chapter Five
Oaths

I arrived at Norfolk General Hospital a few minutes ahead of a storm that had come in off the coast. I marched up to the information desk.

"Hi there, what room is Carl staying in?"

The blank look I received spoke to me. I must have looked frazzled; she looked at me kindly. "Carl who? I need a last name honey."

I paused, Dr. Bailey had given me his last name earlier.

"Oh, his last name is Salem. He uh... came in last night in an ambulance. I talked to a Dr. Bailey about him around an hour ago."

She started typing on her keyboard, her kind look started to fade and she looked back to me.

"Mhmm, go sit over there for me."

She pointed to some chairs. I did as she instructed and waited. The wall in the waiting room was painted with a large mural. It depicted hands reaching up towards a heart with wings. It was a beautiful mural. After a few minutes, two security guards walked into the atrium.

A short time later, a woman with blonde hair gathered up in a ponytail walked up. She was wearing a white coat - I assumed she was a doctor.

"Hi, Mr. Anth?" She said reaching her hand out to me.

"Yeah, yes, hi! Call me Domonic, thanks." I shook her hand nervously, a worried look clearly plastered on my face.

"How's Carl?" I blurted out, assuming she would know how he was doing. She took a deep breath and turned slightly.

"If you follow me, I'll take you to him. He is getting the best care we can give him. He seems to be stable right now, but the accident was hard on him. He has been intermittently conscious over the last 24 hours. He's been very worried about you - he indicated to us that you had been abducted." Her pause had questions in it.

"Right, I was. They must have thought I was someone else. They got halfway to nowhere and abandoned the car with me in the trunk. I eventually got out and took their car to get back here as fast as I could."

She looked relieved.

"I'm glad your calm, it sounds terrifying to me. Carl doesn't know you're here. I didn't want to tell him you had called in case you didn't show up," she paused. "I should have, it would have been better for his health. He's been very worried about you." She smiled at me. "The police are here too, to take his statement, and probably yours now too. I was just going to let them know you had called when I heard Carl had a visitor. I thought you would best be able to explain what happened."

I just wanted to make sure Carl was safe first, then the police.

He saw me enter as I came around the door frame to his room. Carl's eyes shot wide and he scrambled to try and get out of bed, getting tangled in tubes and wires. Panic and relief played across his face.

"Mr. Anth! You're okay! I saw those men take you!" He sagged and fell into me. I caught and held onto him.

"Carl, it's okay. I'm okay. Those guys who took me pulled a disappearing act."

A police officer was standing off to the side. He had tanned skin, a fiery red mane of hair tied into a man-bun, and his eyes were a light shade of brown - almost a dull orange. His badge read "A. Reis" We helped Carl back to bed, then I reached out to shake the officer's hand.

"Mr. Anth, I'm Officer Reis. Carl called us and reported you as being abducted when he woke up in the hospital." Officer Reis shifted his footing and took out a pen.

"I came down to take a statement from him. Seeing that you are no longer in immediate danger, I would like to ask you some questions about the men who took you."

He pulled out a notepad, motioning for me to come out into the hall with him.

I nodded and followed him.

"Carl and I were driving, and a moving truck came out of nowhere and hit us on the passenger side. I was knocked out. I rubbed at my forehead, remembering the decanter flying toward my head.

"The next thing I knew, I had these two men standing over me, and they threw me in a trunk of their rust bucket of a car." I was frustrated and afraid, the memory seemed more offensive to me than it had when it happened. My face must have reflected how I was feeling. Officer Reis had a raised eyebrow and was looking at me awkwardly.

"Anyway, the next thing I knew, I could hear them getting out and running away. I managed to kick open the tail light and see that it was dark out on a dirt road. The car was still running, and no one was around. I found the emergency pull-thingy in the trunk and got myself free." I left out the parts about my body being possessed - I didn't need to sound crazy.

"I checked my phone and I was fairly close to a resort-slash-casino that I hold an account with. I guess at the time I just wanted somewhere familiar. I went there and passed out in the room, got some new clothes, and came back here right after that." He kept jotting down notes; he was very attentive.

"And can you describe them to me?" He looked hopeful, but I couldn't really call up any memory of what they looked like.

"I took a decanter to the head during the accident. It's all pretty blurry until I got out of the trunk." I shrugged, I tried to think of their faces, their voices. It all felt so far away.

"I'm sorry, I can't recall much detail." Officer Reis nodded and handed me a card.

"If you remember anything later, please call me. Maybe get checked out yourself - you could have a concussion. I'll be available any time."

He shook my hand again and walked out towards the elevators. I looked back towards Carl's room and tucked the card into my pocket. When I re-entered the room, Carl was sitting on the edge of his bed. He looked pensive as he raised his gaze up to me.

"Mr. Anth, those men... did they hurt you?"

"Carl, first, call me Domonic, and second, I am here to make sure *you* are okay." He relaxed visibly and looked disappointed in himself.

"I'm sorry I failed you, Mr A-... Domonic. In all the years I worked for your uncle, I didn't have one incident. I was in charge of his safety and his transportation, and now yours. All that time, nothing, and now… this." He hands gestured to IV line and a contraption on his finger, then broadly to the hospital room.

"You were in charge of his safety? What do you mean by that?"

Carl looked at me and rubbed his hands together.

"When he hired me, it was to ensure his personal security, and to ensure his transportation was taken care of - anywhere he wanted to go." He leaned back and set his head on the pillow.

"So, I should fire you and hire someone else? I don't think anyone could have stopped a moving truck from smashing into the side of the car." He shook his head a little as I said it.

"I know sir, I just, I-I'll work to ensure your safety at all times. I promise."

I slapped my forehead, and instantly regretted it as my headache rang back.

"Ooh… Ow. Listen, Carl, stop with the sir stuff. How bad are you hurt?"

He shrugged and held a stern, focused face before speaking. "Not that bad."

The nurse came in. "Hello Carl, it's time for your medicine!" She came up to the side of the bed and gave me a look that said scram.

"Carl, I'll get a room near the hospital and come back in the morning. We're going to be spending a lot of time together - we should get used to each other hanging around!" Carl nodded then looked to the nurse and took the handful of pills she was holding out for him, and I left.

At least he was safe for now. I walked through the lobby on the way to the parking lot, and I ran into the police officer again.

"Mr. Anth, I was reviewing the notes I have here. I didn't want to keep you from visiting your employee, but I would like to ask, where is the car that you were abducted in?"

I sighed. "Right, that's probably important. It's out in the parking lot; I'll take you to it."

I ordered a rideshare as we walked to the lot. I would have to get a rental or something soon. I couldn't drive around an evidence car or wait on drivers all the time. Unless it was Carl, of course. I'd wait for Carl.

"Here it is, Officer Reis. Just as shitty and rusty as it was before. I have a few items of my own in there, can I get them out?"

He responded with a nod and called in for a tow truck. When he was done, he turned to me.

"Mr. Anth, do you have any identification on you?"

I took out my license and handed it to him. He copied the information into his notepad.

"You're extremely lucky to be alright, you know that don't you?" He handed my license back to me with a cocked eyebrow.

I smiled a stupid smile, the same damn smile that was on my face in the casino. "I know. I guess the shock of it hasn't settled in for me yet. I think I just need some sleep and peace before I start worrying about it. I know Carl is safe now, and that's been a huge distraction."

"Well and good then, that's your ride, I assume," he said, pointing over my shoulder.

I turned to look and there it was, a black Mercedes. I shook Officer Reis' hand again and hopped in the car.

I don't even remember the ride to the hotel.

I walked into my room and fell on the bed. I felt like I hadn't slept in two days. I ached. I felt a hole in the core of my being, like I had been stamped with a cookie cutter in the centre of my chest. I just wanted to sleep and feel normal again. I tossed my suit bag, old clothes, and the case of money on one side of the bed and crashed on the other. It didn't take long before I was completely unconscious.

"Son, pour him some wine." The voice echoed. It sounded distant.

I struggled to open my eyes.

"Yes Father…" A younger voice answered.

"Domonic, are you alright?" The voice struck a chord in me - it was the man who had taken control of my body.

My eyes shot open. I was surrounded by a serene group of people, all of them sitting at a tremendous table in the centre of a grove. An older man and woman sat at the heads of the table. Thin white trees surrounded the clearing, providing dappled shade, and a white fog whispered around the edges of the clearing.

I took a deep breath, I could smell the fresh air, but it didn't smell quite right. Like it wasn't really there, like a memory. To my right sat the man who had saved me from my abductors and had controlled my body at the casino. He poured a glass of wine and set it in front of me.

"Here my friend. Drink, rest, relax."

I took a slow drink. It was a complex flavor of different fruits. A faint smoky aftertaste would have ruined it if it weren't for the wonderful addition of honey. It was just as delicious as the wine he had given me at the wake. I realized that almost everyone who was sitting at this table had been at the wake. A chill ran up my spine.

"Where am I?" My voice cut through clear as a bell, no echo, no distance. "And who are all of you?"

They shared meaningful looks between one another, like parents before they explain one of life's lessons to a child. The man at the head of the table nodded to the man beside me.

"I am Dionysus, and this is my family. We all knew your uncle very well. I appreciate your cooperation the other night - I did try to be gentle."

Most of the others giggled at his remark. Not the older woman at the other end of the table, though. She looked at me with an expression of disregard. She turned her gaze back on her wine.

Dionysus continued. "You are a vessel. Your bloodline carries the ability to return us to the mortal coil. There are so few bloodlines left; when your uncle passed, the various families agreed that we could manifest for the funeral, the wake, and for a few days beyond. The agreement ended with the sunrise yesterday, and we were all sent home."

My mind could not rationalize what I was hearing. I tried to convince myself that I had to be dreaming - it was the only thing that made sense.

"You know you're dreaming. Your brain is trying to rationalize what happened to you."

His voice spelled out my thoughts in front of me. I felt cold all over, a mixture of fear and anger. I demanded my mind and body wake up. I closed my eyes, screaming in my mind *"WAKE UP!"*

I opened my eyes again. I was staring at the ceiling of my hotel room. I sighed. It was almost three in the morning, and I didn't feel any more rested. I rolled over and closed my eyes again. I slept, and thankfully, I didn't dream any more that night.

I was woken up by the sound of someone knocking forcefully on my door. I ignored it, wanting more rest, but I was fully jolted awake when the door opened, and two housekeeping staff came in.

"Excuse me! I'm still in here!"

They both looked as shocked as I was, and rushed out of the room. I turned to check the time, and was surprised to see that it was 12:13 pm. I got up, quickly cleaned myself up, and changed into my suit, wearing a t-shirt in lieu of a proper dress shirt. I gathered my things and left the room. I dropped the room keys at the front desk and apologized for my late checkout.

The front desk clerk didn't seem particularly bothered by it.

I tried to get a rideshare service to pick me up, but all the time quotes were tremendous, probably because it was around lunchtime. I looked around outside to evaluate my options. As luck would have it, a taxi was coming by. I waved, and he pulled over.

"Where you wanna go?" He asked. A thick black mustache bobbed up and down as he talked.

"Norfolk General, please." I got in the back seat and we were off. I busied myself on my phone, trying to not pay attention to the fortune in my suitcase. I looked around the cab, feeling a little anxious about it now.

"Hey, is there a car dealership around here?" The cab driver nodded and took an exit. Fifteen minutes later, I paid him and was walking through the lot of a car dealership connected to a strip mall. I couldn't see any specific signage. I was starting to think it was a used car lot.

I was approached by a salesperson almost immediately. He had slick hair and a fine suit that carried a thick cloud of cologne in it. I shook his hand and smiled, quickly jumping ahead of his sales pitch.

"Good afternoon, I'd like to speak with the shift manager for the sales staff." He looked confused and his eyes went up and down, apparently evaluating my suit.

"Hi, alright, yeah, come with me inside. I'll take you to Kevin."

We walked in, and he showed me a waiting area, then headed upstairs. He came back down a few minutes later, bringing with him a middle-aged man with a fair complexion and very fine light red hair in a short, neat cut. He approached with hand outstretched.

"Hello sir, my name is Kevin. Desmond here told me you'd like to see me. What can I do for you?"

His voice had the high flat tone of nasal congestion. I shook his hand and stood up, glancing at Desmond only briefly.

"Hi, Kevin. Call me Domonic. Can you tell me who the best salesperson is? I want to know who makes the most money selling vehicles."

Kevin motioned to Desmond.

"Desmond has been our top performer for the last four months in a row."

"Desmond, in your opinion, who is the worst performer?"

He looked at Kevin, and then back to me. I immediately knew that Kevin was the worst salesperson here.

"I uh, I don't have access to that information."

Kevin visibly relaxed as Desmond's words left his mouth. I smiled that foreign smile and hefted my suitcase.

"Kevin, would you please show me around the lot? I'd like to make a purchase."

Kevin was very pleasant, chatting amicably as he showed me around the lot. He had a story for every vehicle, and you could tell he really loved cars. He asked the standard questions about what kind of car I was looking for, and with a gleam in his eye, led me around the building. As I rounded the corner, I laid eyes on a gorgeous black car. It was sleek and luxurious. Kevin pulled the keys out of his pocket and opened the front door for me.

I carefully went through everything in the vehicle. It had an extremely comfortable leather interior. The front had plush seats and a luxury storage compartment in between them. The car could sit eight people, with two benches in the back that faced each other that could seat three each. I spent some time sitting in each seat. When I climbed into the back, I immediately noticed a small shelf for drinks to be set in. I liked it.

"Kevin, let's take it for a test drive."

He was quick to accommodate my request. Just a few minutes later we were on our way.

"So, do you like luxury vehicles, or do you drive for a living?"

Kevin looked uncomfortable. I could see why his awkward nature might turn people off.

"No, I don't drive for a living. I want to get this for a friend."

Kevin guffawed. "Jeez I wish I had a friend to buy me cars!" He giggled awkwardly. He must have thought I was joking.

The vehicle seemed to drive and handle fine to me, so I turned around and headed back to the dealership.

"Kevin, let's do up some paperwork. I'll take it."

Kevin seemed very excited, trying a little too hard to play it cool.

"Sure, come with me. I'll be happy to take care of this for you. There is an insurance place in the strip mall too. If you want, I can make a call for you. The manager over there is pretty tight with me."

We made it up the stairs to his cramped office. There were stacks of boxes everywhere.

"Sorry about the boxes, the sales team moved them in here so they could have a smoking room."

I flinched at that. "Oh yeah? That's nice of you."

He pulled out a folder and started typing away on his keyboard.

"Okay, so we have the luxury edition - that has all the bells and whistles. What color do you want it in?"

I paused and raised my hand.

"Kevin, I want the one we drove. Insured and plated today."

His eyes popped open.

"Oh, I see. I didn't expect that you'd want it today. Of course, sir. We should talk about financing then. Do you have a down payment amount in mind?"

I lifted my suitcase onto the table.

"How much is the vehicle if I wanted to pay cash - no financing?"

Kevin raised his eyebrows but didn't look up and continued typing.

"Okay, well, if you wanted to buy the vehicle outright, without financing, the entire thing after tax comes to $78,768. There are a bunch of add-ons and upsells here too that you can have if you want."

I closed my eyes and nodded.

"Yeah go ahead, add it all on - maintenance plans, roadside programs, anything you have. Tack it on there."

His forehead furrowed as went back to clicking on the keyboard.

"Well alright. It comes up to $83,945 now."

I opened my briefcase and looked at the money, I was overwhelmed for a moment. Sitting there holding a fortune in my lap. They were put together in packets of $10,000 wrapped with convenient numbered bands.

"Alright, I'm going to go use the washroom. Can I leave my briefcase here? And can you please call and get that insurance and plate sorted out for me?"

He picked up the phone and winked at me. It was so awkward.

I headed back down the stairs.

"Desmond?" I waved him over. "Hey, I'm up there trying to figure something out. I want to get a car. There are a ton of boxes in there. What's the deal?"

His face broke out in the biggest shit-eating grin I had ever seen.

"Oh, yeah. There was this big-ass storage room, but we wanted a smoke room and it was jam-packed with those boxes. He just kind of let us put them in there."

I tried to force my laugh to sound sincere. "That is hilarious. Where is the bathroom?"

He pointed to a small hallway, and I headed that way. It was near a row of tiny, little office. I went to the bathroom and took care of business. A short while later, I walked back to the call floor, preparing to go finalize with Kevin.

"Hey, dude, what's Kevin selling you?" Desmond called out.

"The black car out there." I pointed.

"Oh yeah, that's a sweet model. So, I don't know what kind of package he is working up for you, but I could probably get you a better deal. Kevin isn't really that good with the system."

I held my chin thoughtfully. I noticed a couple of other sales reps standing near the reception desk, and casually walked over that way. Desmond followed.

"Kevin is the sales manager, isn't he? I figured he'd be able to get me the best deal."

Desmond poorly stifled a laugh behind his hand. I couldn't stand the guy.

"Oh yeah, he probably used to be good at this, but since most of us have been around, he's just been a floater, helping with paperwork and getting coffees."

We had made it within earshot of the other salespeople.

I spoke just a little too loudly. "Well Desmond, Kevin has been more than fantastic. I'm not sure if you can give me a better deal, and I don't particularly care. I prefer solid customer service over a slightly better price. Thanks though."

I walked away, hoping that someone had heard what I said and cared that someone had a positive thought about Kevin. I climbed back up the stairs to his office.

"Yes, that's right, if you don't mind. I'll have someone stopping by for that right away. Why yes! Thank you! Mhmm, okay. Bye now!" He set down the phone receiver.

I sat down and reopened my briefcase. He hadn't touched it. This guy was a good soul - I could feel it.

"Alright, Mr. Anth, your insurance and plate should be ready by the time we're done. I just sent an email over to Shelly at the reception desk. She's going to run and pick it up for you. I've added the amount to your final invoice, so you don't need to head down into the mall."

I smiled, and it was *my* smile.

"Kevin, how much is all of this going to cost now?"

He flipped through some notes and puckered his lips in thought.

"Everything should come to $84,795."

"Great, just great. That sounds a little light for the insurance though."

"You are correct. I only got you a 7-day insurance plan, so you can transfer it over to your own insurance company."

"That's perfect. Thanks very much, Kevin."

"How did you want to process this today? I have a few different options."

I chuckled and grabbed nine tidy packets of money. "I'll pay cash. Here is $90,000. You can keep the change. I want you to do something for me though. Stop letting Desmond steal your sales. You are good at this - you're not trying to sell me things I don't want or need."

The look that landed in Kevin's eyes was chilly.

"What makes you think that Desmond is stealing my sales?"

I was a surprised by the change in his tone . "On my way out of the bathroom, he called me over and asked me to buy from him. He said he'd get me a better deal. Frankly, I don't care what I pay for the car. Money isn't exactly a concern for me right now, but I thought it was a really shitty thing to do."

I could see a vein in his neck pulsating and throbbing. He took a few deep breaths.

"Thank you for telling me. I'll have to chat with him about that."

He took the money and handed me my sales documents to sign. He tucked the neatly into a folder and handed them to me and walked me back down the stairs. When we arrived in the lobby, I shook his hand, took the keys, and winked at Desmond on my way out.

Time to surprise Carl with a new car!

I walked into the hospital room while Carl was working on his supper.

"Hey Carl, sorry I didn't get here sooner. I had to pick something up."

With his mouth full of food, he raised his eyebrows and waved me in. I took a seat.

"I'm sorry to interrupt your dinner. Here, look at this."

I held up my phone and showed him a picture of the new car. He looked confused. I put the phone away and brought up the suitcase.

"Here, open this."

I set it on the side of his bed and he opened it. Inside was $127,000, the new car keys, and all the sales information.

His eyes went wide. He swallowed his mouthful.

"Domonic, what is this? I can't accept this!"

I waved him off.

"I won the money, and I already have enough. I don't know how much you get paid. The keys are for a new car I got for you - the one in the photo. I've been thinking about it, and when you're ready to go, all released from the hospital and everything, I'd like to travel back to Seattle with you."

He looked relieved, anxious, excited, and happy all at the same time.

"That sounds really nice, Domonic. I swore an oath to your uncle when he was alive that I'd keep you safe for as long as I could. I felt so broken up when you got abducted. I'm going to keep you safe from now on. I swear the same oath to you now."

I had to pause and drink in the peace of the moment. He was intensely focused and so serious. I couldn't tell if he was in pain; I didn't want to know if he was. I knew this was extremely important to him and I respected that.

"Thank you, Carl. Right now, let's focus on getting you hale and healthy."

He looked down at the pills on his table, and at the food on his plate. He threw the pills in the trash, looked at me, and went back to eating his food.

"Less pain medication will help me know where I'm hurting."

I nodded slowly. "Sounds good Carl."

Chapter Six
Mind Over Matter

"Excellent work, Carl. I can't believe how much progress you've made over the last few days."

Dr. Bailey was pleased with him, and for good reason. It was remarkable how much he had improved.

Carl grunted in agreement. He was lifting more weight than I thought I could, and it was part of his physical therapy.

"How are you feeling?" She asked him, watching the barbells go up and down. He racked them and wiped his face with a towel.

"I feel good," he said, but winced as he turned and sat down.

She listened to his heart, his breathing, and checked his blood pressure.

"I think we can get you out of here now. Do you have any pain?"

He shook his head and threw his hands out to the side.

"I think I'm okay. Nothing hurts that much."

She spent a moment appraising him. "I'm going to recommend that you get in touch with a physiotherapist to help with stiffness and get you back to 100%."

Carl smiled and looked up at her.

"Thank you, Dr. Bailey; I'll keep that in mind."

He reached out to her, they shook hands, and she left the room. I watched his eyes follow her out.

"Carl, why don't you ask her to get some coffee?"

He abashedly rubbed his head. "No, no. She's a busy doctor, and we have places to be."

The knock at the door pulled our attention. A nurse came in and walked through the discharge papers with Carl. He signed them, and she left. He looked around the room, biting his lip, pensive.

"Alright, well, maybe I'll see if she wants to get a quick coffee. We can leave later today."

I shook my head. "Or tomorrow, or the next day, or whenever. I'm in no rush."

He put on the rest of his clothing and stepped out of the room. A few minutes later, he came back in and nodded to me.

"She's done at three, wants to meet me at a café nearby."

I gave him a thumbs up and got out of my chair.

"Alright, let's head back to the hotel and get you a room so you can get cleaned up."

Carl whistled when he saw the car. "Nice car! Do you mind if we stop by the impound lot? They have our bags still."

I popped open the passenger door. "Not a problem. I'm going to ride up front for a little bit if you don't mind."

He got in and let out a contented sigh. "This is a hell of a nice ride. Thank you for finding a replacement."

I adjusted my seat and fiddled with the climate controls for the passenger side. I shrugged. "Well, we need a ride and man, I kind of just walked into the money for it. Once we're back at the hotel, I'll just hang out there until you're ready to go. Then, we'll make our way to Seattle."

He nodded. "Awesome," he paused. "I appreciate you pushing me to talk to Dr. Bailey - uh - Samantha. She's very nice."

I chuckled. "Yeah? Good. I hope you two have a nice time together."

An hour later we were back at the hotel. I laid down on the couch in my room.

~

The café smelled wonderful. The kitchen was busy baking. The aroma of cinnamon buns and roasting coffee beans was heavenly. Carl took a deep breath in and sighed. A waitress walked up to Carl and looked at the empty seat.

"You doing alright hon? Can I bring you anything?"

Carl smiled abashedly and shrugged.

"I am - just a little nervous. I'm waiting for someone, I'll be fine until she gets here."

The waitress tapped her notepad with her pen. "Alright. I'll be back in a little bit." She moved on to the next table.

Samantha walked through the door in a stunning pastel blue summer dress. Her hair was blonde, curled, and framed her face down to her shoulders. She waved and came over, smiling. Carl drank in the image of her, imprinting it in his mind. She was radiant, almost as tall as he was as he stood and reached out to shake her hand.

"Hello! You look great!"

She blushed and cleared her throat. "You look quite nice yourself, now that you're not in a hospital gown."

He chuckled and smoothed his hands down the front of his shirt.

"Yes, well, thankfully I have recovered not only in health but in fashion."

They both laughed.

Samantha looked up as a waitress approached the table.

"Good afternoon, what can I get you two?"

Carl motioned for Samantha to order first.

"I will take a blonde roast. One cream, and one sugar."

The waitress looked to Carl.

"Uh, I'll have a black coffee."

She left to get their drinks, returning a few minutes later. They thanked her and took their drinks, each taking slow, gentle sips and enjoying the comfortable atmosphere.

"So, Carl, how long are you in town?" She looked over the rim of her cup as she drank.

"Not long. Domonic and I are headed to Seattle tomorrow, I think, or maybe the day after."

Her eyes flashed wider for a very brief moment. "What are your plans for the rest of the day?" She looked up at him inquisitively, biting her lower lip.

"I've got nothing planned. I'm all yours." He held his hands open. He met her eyes, and they gazed at each other for a lingering moment.

She cleared her throat and put her drink down. She reached into her purse and pulled out a ten dollar bill, set it on the table, and looked back at Carl.

"Why don't we go somewhere else?"

Carl set his drink down next to hers and took her by the hand, leading her outside. Nearing the car, he paused and turned to her.

"Samantha, I'm not used to… this-"

She interrupted him. "Neither am I. Listen. I work 80-hour weeks. I don't get out much. I hate using hook-up apps, and I'm the unique position of knowing you are in really good… health. I just think this is win-win for the both of us."

Carl raised an eyebrow and laughed. He appreciated her direct honesty.

"Samantha, would you like to go back to my hotel room?"

She leaned in and kissed him, then pulled away to look him in the eyes.

"Yes, Carl. I think I would."

~

The next morning, I went downstairs to check out the hotel's little breakfast spread. I found Dr. Bailey and Carl sitting together having coffee.

"Morning Carl, Dr. Bailey." I nodded to them as I walked by to get my own coffee and a newspaper.

"Good morning, Mr. Anth." She beat Carl to the greeting.

"Hi Domonic. How was your night?"

I stirred vanilla creamer into a cup of coffee as I turned back to them.

"Not bad. I slept quite well actually. How about you two?"

They shared the same embarrassed look. Clearly, they hadn't slept very much.

"Well, I'll be heading back upstairs. I am heading out later to get a few things for the trip to Seattle. We can leave tomorrow or the day after."

They looked at each other, exchanging whispers, and then Carl looked back to me. He looked torn.

"Sounds good. So, do you - uh - will you be needing me for anything today?"

I shook my head. "No, it's all good. I'm going to use a rideshare today. I'm going to get ready to go. Thanks though."

The happy couple got up and quickly made their way to the elevators. I went back to my room and got cleaned up.

A short while later, I was in a silver S.U.V. pulling up to a big box store. I went inside and got myself a new phone for my current number, and a second phone with a new number.

"Was there anything else I could help you with sir?"

The man behind the counter seemed genuinely eager to help with anything I needed.

"Yes, actually. I need a couple of laptops, bags, power banks, and an in-vehicle inverter."

"Of course! Come with me, sir."

I went with the sales rep. We got everything picked out and ready to go. I paid the man and awaited my rideshare - it was the same silver jeep as before. I headed back to the hotel and spent the rest of the day configuring the new laptops and phones. It was nice to spend a day in. I went to bed early. I still felt exhausted. I figured I must still be recovering from all the... excitement... over the last few days. I had a feeling Carl was having a much more entertaining night than I was.

~

Beep beep beep

Her pager went off right in the middle of the best part of the night.

"Shit! Sorry, one second."

Samantha looked at her pager and sighed. "Carl, I have to go to work."

Carl shifted in bed, propping himself up on his elbow.

"I'm going to miss your bedside manners, Samantha."

She looked over her shoulder and pouted at Carl.

"I enjoyed getting to know you." She grasped his hand and squeezed, and he squeezed back. He watched her get dressed, moving to get comfortable, and winced. It wasn't the first time he had winced during their time together.

"Carl, you really should reconsider my offer of something to manage your pain. I don't know how you can stand it." She looked worried.

"You gave me the best pain management." His smile was charming and flawless. "Besides, it's good to know where I'm hurting. It helps me move and heal in ways that work for what I want to do, and what I enjoy doing." He smiled suggestively.

"Oh? You are so bad!" Her laughter was soothing to Carl, and a sigh escaped him. He was going to miss her.

"Really though, Samantha, it's just mind over matter. I can endure some pain in order to feel the good things in life. Painkillers just leave me numb to it all." Carl got up and walked to her, embracing her in a hug. "Go save lives. It was nice to meet you."

She held him tightly and rested her head on his shoulder. "Thank you for this. It's been very cathartic."

Beep beep beep

Carl giggled at the beeping. "You better run."

She reached up and kissed him, then pulled away and smiled.

"Bye Carl."

She turned and left, closing the door softly behind her.

Carl crawled back into bed. "Bye Samantha."

~

"No Dr. Bailey this morning?" I looked around, noticing the lack of the good doctor.

Carl sighed, looking down at his breakfast.

"No, she had to go to work last night. She's a good woman." He stretched and grunted in pain.

"There is nothing saying you need to come with me, you know. You could stay here. You've got a nice little nest egg in that suitcase."

Carl shook his head. "No. It was fun, but I don't think we could make a relationship work. I'm too clingy."

I laughed. I couldn't help it. He laughed too.

"Well, alright then. I'll go get my things and meet you at the front desk."

He finished his breakfast and went to gather his belongings. A short time later we were hitting the road.

"I have missed the road." Carl ran his hands on the wheel, looking more comfortable as the moments went by.

"Well, I've missed home. I guess I'll have to settle somewhere. For now, I just want to go home."

My mind drifted to the dream I had the other night. I had been starting to toy with the idea that it had been more than just a dream. Or, maybe, it was all part of some kind of mental breakdown caused by the stress of the abduction. I had no idea. I wanted to leave it behind me, but it kept cropping up in my mind when I wasn't actively thinking about something else.

"Carl, is there anything you can tell me about my uncles' lifestyle? Anything way out of the ordinary?"

I waited through a long stretch of silence. It was abruptly broken by his strained voice.

"I... can't. Your uncle forbade me from ever discussing what took place in his life. I can't betray his trust. I'm sorry."

I couldn't fault him for it, but I wished I could know more.

"It's alright Carl. I won't press the issue. Thank you for being honest with me."

He relaxed, and we kept cruising down the road.

As we drove, I sent an email to Mr. Donovan explaining what had happened over the last week. I wanted him to be kept in the loop, and it felt like the right thing to do.

"Do you have many dealings with Mr. Donovan?" I asked Carl.

He shook his head. "No, I hadn't met him until your uncle passed away. Before then, the only times I had heard of him was when your uncle spoke with him on the phone."

I chewed on that for a little while. "Carl, how long did you work for my uncle?"

He thought about it and turned to me briefly when he answered. "Would have been thirteen years next month."

That was longer than I'd thought. "That is quite a long service record. Did he pay - do I pay you well?"

Carl nodded enthusiastically. "Oh, yes. I get three grand a week, after tax, benefits, and a variety of perks. It's been quite a wonderful position."

I agreed with him. It seemed like a pretty awesome gig. "That's awesome. I'm taking it you and my uncle weren't exactly friends though?"

"That's an understatement. No, your uncle believed in a certain level of professional distance. There were a few nights a year where we'd let our hair down and cut loose. Other than that, we kept our relationship relatively professional."

I could see the benefit of that kind of arrangement. "I see. I hope you don't mind that I'm friendlier than that. I like sitting up front more than I like sitting in the back."

He nodded as I spoke. "Absolutely. It would be a nice change of pace to be friends with my employer."

I liked the idea of forging a friendship with Carl more and more.

After a few hours of driving, Carl's phone rang. He slipped in an earpiece, reached out to the dashboard and tapped a button.

"Hello? Yeah, alright, I'm not far. I'll meet you there. Right. Yeah. Cash? Sounds good... Thanks." He hung up and looked ahead with a serious expression. "I need to stop and pick something up. I placed a call to an acquaintance yesterday; he is going to meet us and give me a few things I need. I hope you don't mind? I won't be long."

I was curious, but I just shrugged. "You do you, Carl. It's all good."

I had butterflies from hearing his end of the conversation, but I told myself I had to trust him, so I kept my mouth shut and tried to relax.

Not long after, Carl pulled onto a side road and pulled up next to a box truck. The truck had a logo for a catering company on the side. He looked at me.

"Wait here. I'll be right back."

He left the car running, grabbed the suitcase from the trunk and walked around the back of the catering truck. I couldn't see or hear what he was doing. Less than a minute later, Carl walked back out with his suitcase and a large black pelican case. He spent some time moving things around in the trunk, slammed it shut, and then got back in. He pulled away and headed back to the main road.

"Sorry about that. I wanted to get some protection for us in case anyone else tries to abduct you in the future."

"Protection?" The question was bait. I assumed he had just bought a gun from the back of that truck, but I wanted to be sure. I realized that I hadn't really put any thought into Carl's role as security in my life.

"Yes. It's easy enough to get licensed weapons, but your uncle made it very clear to me that he did not want me to have anything licensed or registered. If I ever needed to use one, it should be destroyed as soon as possible. It took a few years to streamline the process, but now I can typically get almost any weapon in a day or two. If I ever need to destroy one, I can do that as well."

I was stunned. It sounded like my uncle might have had more uses for Carl than I thought.

"So, what did you get?" I didn't know if it was appropriate to ask or not.

"Two Beretta M9's, eight clips, 400 subsonic rounds, and two suppressors. I don't know if you've had any firearm training. I insisted your uncle learn how to properly use my weapons, so that he could defend himself if necessary. I insist the same for you. When we get to some isolated areas, we'll do a little training and practice."

I had never held a gun, much less fired one.

"Wait - you bought *me* a gun?"

He chuckled derisively. "No, those are both for me. If you want to carry a gun, I can arrange for you to have one, although then you might not need me around!" He winked and winced as he laughed.

"Still not one hundred percent?"

He relaxed in his seat with a shit-eating grin. "Oh… Samantha put me through my paces, but I'm roadworthy."

The implication was salacious. I had to stop myself from laughing like a schoolboy.

"Fair enough. At least she was thorough with you."

The road opened up before us as we approached the I-94 west. We sighed contentedly at seeing the open road. It felt good to be out of the city. I enjoyed the quiet hum of the tires on the pavement. I could almost feel the world move beneath us as we made our way west. It was peaceful. I laid my head back and closed my eyes.

~

I was dreaming. I could feel the grass between my toes. My eyes opened to reveal the garden and the dining table again. There was only one man at the table now. He sat near the head of the table at the corner and was examining a crystal glass half filled with red wine.

"Hello again, Dionysus. What can I do for you?"

I was starting to get used to his presence. He was charming and kind. I was pretty sure he had saved my life, and I had trouble finding a reason not to like him.

He smiled and motioned to a chair next to him. "Sit, my friend. I am here to answer some questions for you. I am sure you have some, since our trip to the Casino."

His voice echoed and felt distant to me.

I sat quickly. I had so many questions that it was hard to know where to start. I looked at him excitedly.

"What happened that night?"

"I saved you, although I don't know from whom. You embraced me, which allowed me to enter your body. I then made good use of my time by going to that casino and having a wonderful night." He paused and took another sip of his wine. "Anything else?"

I laughed and strained to not pay attention to the craziness of it all.

"Yes. Why jump into my body? You do have a body of your own, right? I saw you - all of you - at the funeral."

He set his glass down and took a deep breath. "We did then, but we don't have permanent forms now. I'll try to explain it as simply as I can." He filled his glass and drank deeply from it. "A very long time ago, the elders in each of our families agreed to bar passage to the mortal coil. Your kind refers to this barrier as 'the veil' and I suppose the name fits well enough. It can only be brought down if every elder agrees to it."

He paused for another drink. I noticed the fog shift and move from side to side. Dionysus also seemed to notice, but continued.

"Your uncle was prolific. Of all the vessels we've ever known, he was the most driven and committed human that has ever worked with us. The elders agreed that they would take the veil down for seven days so that we could enter your world and celebrate Michelle."

I straightened myself. My eyes bore into Dionysus.

"I need to know, what would have happened if I didn't come to the funeral? I've been wondering about it. You know, I wasn't very close to my uncle."

Dionysus shrugged and ran his hand through his hair. "We knew of you from Michelle. There is no way for us to know who a vessel is anymore. The bloodlines are all but gone, and you are the last of your line. Although, we are hoping you might choose to haver children, perhaps someone to carry on your duties as a vessel." He paused and leaned forward. "But you *are* bound to us. My family would be able to sense you anywhere in the world. If you decided to not attend Michelle's funeral and wake, we would have come to you."

I heard my name echo in from deep in the fog as it shifted again from side to side.

"What's happening?"

"Soon you're going to wake up. Someone is shaking you," he explained. "As I was saying, we came to your world for a few days to honor your uncle Michelle. The veil has been restored now, and we again rely on you to be our vessel so that we may enter your world."

I stood up, and everything started to slowly spin. My chair tumbled back toward the tree line, then moved forward again to rest against me. Dionysus sipped from his glass, his seat unmoving. The trees bent inward towards us and the fog rushed in. They struck against me, and in a moment it was black.

I woke to Carl calling my name and shaking my shoulder gently.

"Domonic, time get up. We are going to train now."

I looked past him out the window. Cans were set up on a few rocks.

"Great, just let me stretch." I yawned.

~

"Alright, take your time and breathe. Your stance is good, your posture is good. Just aim, breathe, squeeze."

The combination of the subsonic ammunition and the suppressor made the shot so quiet we didn't need hearing protection. When I squeezed, there was very little resistance. I felt it kick in my hands. The heat from the shot registered only briefly. A huge smile sprung up on my face when I saw the can flip off the top of the rock.

"Very good! Now secure your weapon."

I moved with deliberate intention, making sure my finger was clear of the trigger and clicking the safety. I put the gun down.

"You're doing quite well. I'll set up a few more targets. I want you to walk towards them while you shoot this time. Your motivation to succeed: if you fail to hit all the targets before you empty your clip, you will spend one hour walking naked alongside the car."

I looked at him in disbelief. "Really?"

He nodded giving me a dead serious stare. I looked at the gun in front of me.

"Can I have a fresh magazine?"

Carl laughed at me. "Eight cans require eight rounds. Fourteen is generous!" he exclaimed as he walked around, setting up his targets.

I stood at the ready and didn't respond. He finished setting up eight empty cans, then turned and smirked at me. "Very good! Ready... Go!"

I walked forward slowly, taking my shots in time with my steps. It was awkward walking and shooting at the same time. I was please with myself, knocking down three cans in a row. Hit, hit, hit! A confident smile snuck onto my face, and I lost my focus. The fourth can took three attempts to knock down. Miss, miss, hit! The fourth one took another three. Miss, miss, hit! I took a deep breath and clenched my jaw. I walked towards the last three cans. Hit, hit, hit! I had two rounds left. I ejected the magazine, made sure the chamber was clear, and set them down on the large rock in front of me. I turned to Carl and smiled.

"Looks like I'm not walking naked!"

Carl chuckled and went about cleaning up the debris. I helped him pack it all into a black garbage bag and stash it in the trunk, and then we were on our way again.

"Thanks for the lesson Carl, that was actually pretty fun."

Carl pointed at the glove box. I opened it.

"There is a card in there. If you ever want to really learn how to use a gun, call that number. You can get some really good training on almost any weapon there."

I took out my wallet and put the card inside. "Thanks again."

We rode in silence for a while. I turned my mind to the thoughts of what I was going to need to do in Seattle.

Chapter Seven

Old Life

"And on page seventeen, you'll see that we have increased call flow analysis speed by 11%. Good work on that one, Kyle."

Martin grinned at Kyle with enthusiasm. He was a short, boring man, and his life seemed to revolve around the Friday meetings.

Kyle smiled and nodded his head. He hated these meetings. It was almost over though. Almost.

"Thanks. Thank you."

"That brings the official business to a close. Does anyone have anything they'd like to bring up for discussion?"

Everyone at the table looked around. Neck ties got looser at the end of the week, and glazed eyes waited for the weekend. No one made eye contact but looked around to see if anyone was going to drag this out any longer.

"Very good, then, this meeting is called to a close. There are donuts in the break room. If anyone wants one, help yourself!"

Kyle avoided the donuts and the people. He went through the call floor, all the way to the other side of the building, and out to the smoke break area.

Kyle saw him as soon as he stepped outside. Matthew was sitting on the bench, staring at his phone, and looking absolutely fine. His shirt was snug, showing off the roundness of his shoulders and the firmness of his chest.

"Hey, Matt! On break?"

Matt looked up from his phone and smiled. "Hello. Yeah… just on my first fifteen."

Kyle sat down beside him. "What are you doing this weekend?" Kyle leaned in, feeling the warmth of Matt's shoulder and the slight pressure as Matt leaned back into him.

"Well, I'm planning on just being lazy at home. Maybe watch some movies…" His smile was warm and inviting. "And if you aren't busy, I would love some company."

Kyle was flustered. He hadn't spent any time with Matthew in the last week, and the thought of a weekend with him made his heart race. "I have nothing planned. I should bring something like popcorn." Kyle said, trying to sound casual.

"*Or condoms.*" Matt muttered under his breath.

Kyle didn't hear him "Or maybe some drinks. Was there anything you wanted me to bring?"

Matthew put a hand on Kyle's shoulder. "You don't need to bring anything," he sighed and laid his head on Kyles' shoulder.

"*Kyle, please report to reception.*"

Kyle sighed. "Duty calls. Later, Matt!"

Matthew waved him off and went back to his phone.

"This better be important," Kyle muttered as he headed back in

~

"So, I just want to make sure I have this right. You want to visit your former supervisor, from the job you quit to guarantee your inheritance?"

I nodded with his summary.

"Yeah. He and I were really good friends. I owe him some kind of explanation."

Carl leaned over in his chair and whispered to me. "You are a strange duck. Your uncle Michelle would have approved though."

I was surprised at how much he respected the opinions of my deceased uncle.

 A few minutes later, Kyle came into reception. His face fell when he saw me.

"Hello, Domonic." He crossed his arms and shot daggers at me with his eyes.

"Hey Kyle, thanks for coming out to see me. I just-"

"Yes, well if I had known it was you, I wouldn't have bothered. I was busy. And who is this?"
He turned to Carl.

The interruption raised my hackles.

 Kyle lifted his chin in defiance as Carl stood up and straightened his jacket.

"*I* am his personal bodyguard and driver. And *you* will watch your tone with Mr. Anth." Carl moved a half step closer to Kyle, his eyes issuing a challenge.

"Bodyguard? Driver? What the hell happened to you, Dom? You were going to a funeral. Then, you quit over the phone, without notice, and now you show up again out of the blue. It doesn't make sense." He took a step back from Carl.

I put a hand on Carl's shoulder. "Thank you, Carl, it's alright."

He stepped back.

"Kyle, I can't tell you everything, but things have changed for me. There was a condition. I had to terminate any standing position I held with any company. Immediately, in the presence of a lawyer. I'm sorry."

"You're still an asshole for doing it to me like that. You should have just asked for Martin instead of dropping it on me." Kyle glared at Carl and then at me. "Martin told me I had to do your work until we found a replacement. Do you know how much I *didn't* want that? I'm glad you came out of it smelling like roses, but you are still a grade A asshole." He crossed his arms and stood there waiting.

I walked up to him with my hands out. "I'm sorry Kyle. I can't undo what I did. I had no time to collect my thoughts. We are talking about a massive inheritance here. How about you let me make it up to you? Please."

Kyle looked at Carl and shook his head. He sighed and uncrossed his arms, then rubbed his face. His gaze softened.

"No, its okay man, don't worry about it. Just give me a hug, you prick."

I embraced him. Kyle was my best friend in the world. When we parted, he looked relieved. He straightened his tie and looked at me.

"You know, Nicole has been asking what happened to you. Might be worth giving her a call."

I looked past Kyle, catching a glimpse of the call floor. "Isn't she here?" I asked.

Kyle shrugged. "No. She quit a couple days after you did. She's slinging coffee down near the fish market."

I hadn't thought of Nicole in a few days. Maybe I should go see her.

"Thanks, Kyle. I'll be in town for a few days. I have to figure out what I'm doing. If you find the time, do you want to stop by?"

He shook his head and smiled. "I'm spending the weekend with Matt; we'll be very busy." He cracked a lascivious smirk and waved as he headed back into the call floor.

"He's a little emotional, isn't he?" Carl commented.

"Yeah, he was always a big emotions guy. Just glad that's taken care of. I'll drive next, Carl. You just relax and get ready to meet a couple of my favorite people."

~

Mmmmmrow, mmmmmrow, mmmmrow

Carl was sitting on my couch, petting Coaldust. Ruth was in my recliner. I puttered in the kitchen, making tea.

"Domonic, you know I can't cash that cheque. I know you say you've come into some money, but you need to keep that for yourself, dear."

Over my shoulder, I could see her smiling at Carl and Coaldust.

"Coaldust likes you. I don't know many people who he likes." I watched Coaldust stretch and purr in his lap.

Carl pet him gently "Well, I've never met a cat who liked to go on walks with a leash."

Ruth beamed at the remark. Taking Coaldust for walks was her favorite thing in the world. "He really does! He's a little furry exercise machine!"

They both laughed. I came over with their cups of tea.

"Ruth, I inherited a tremendous amount of money. That cheque is the equivalent to pocket change to me now. I want you to have it. You're pretty much family to me, and besides, Coaldust likes you."

Ruth looked from me to Carl, and she finally gave in.

"I don't know what to say Dommy!" She looked upset. Coaldust sat up and ran to her. He jumped in her lap and rubbed himself against her, purring.

"Oh, Coaldust! I'm going to miss you too!"

I knew I couldn't bring Coaldust with me, wherever I went. I'd be unable to be as attentive.

"Actually Ruth, I was wondering if you'd be willing to adopt Coaldust. I can't have the responsibility of a pet in my life now."

She nodded emphatically, tears welling up in her eyes. "Oh my, yes! I would love to have him in my little life!"

Coaldust licked her on the cheek and rubbed against. She turned her attention back to him. "Yes, I'm sorry Coaldust. I forgot." She reached into her purse and pulled out a treat. He took it carefully and crunched away happily. "A bunch of packages came for you. They're in my apartment. Let me just-"

Carl got up and reached over to her, putting his hand on her shoulder.

"I can get them, Ruth. You relax."

She smiled and blushed.

"Thank you, Carl. They are just inside the door to the right." She waited for her door to open, then whispered to me. "Dommy, your friend is so handsome. Are you and he...?"

I shook my head. "No Ruth, he is a friend and my employee."

She tapped her nose. "Good. Don't dip your pen in the company ink."

I laughed so hard the sound stuck in my throat, and my face and stomach hurt.

"What's so funny?" Carl came in with his arms loaded to his chin with packages.

"Oh... Nothing."

He grunted and side-eyed us as he set the packages on the kitchen table. "These are all from Mr. Donovan."

 I had forgotten about the lockbox and those tiny puzzle pieces.

"Thanks, Carl. Ruth, I'll be sticking around here for a little while. You're welcome to take Coaldust anytime, but do you mind if I have him over here for a night to say goodbye?"

She leaned down and gave Coaldust a kiss on the head. "You enjoy your time with him. If you need anything, I'll be in my apartment. Um. Carl, I wanted to go to the bank later. Would you mind walking me there?"

He nodded. "Of course. Just knock when you're ready. I'll be here with Domonic."

She giggled and headed to her apartment. When I heard her door close, I turned to Carl.

"Looks like you have another Dr. Bailey situation here, Carl."

I turned my attention to the pile of packages and started tearing open the wrapping. This was going to take a while. I turned to ask Carl if he wanted to help, when his phone rang.

"Yes sir, we've made it to Seattle. I don't know how long we'll be here, though."

I listened to his half of the conversation half-heartedly. He wasn't making any effort to make it private.

"No, aside from the incident you were emailed about, things went smoothly. We made it here in good time. We did stop for some target practice though."

I could hear the laughter on the other end of the line. It sounded like Mr. Donovan.

"Very good sir. I will. Thank you. Goodbye." Carl hung up and turned to me. "Mr. Donovan is concerned about your well-being. Because of the abduction, he wants me to send him reports and tell him if anything out of the ordinary is happening." He looked pained.

"Prudent. So long as I am alive, he has a steady source of income. I can't imagine there is anything to worry about now though, right?"

He walked up to the table and picked up an unwrapped parcel. He stared at it apprehensively.

"In all the years I worked for your uncle, no one ever tried to abduct him. No one ever tried to hurt him. But, with you, in the first week of your inheritance, we were ambushed, attacked, and you were abducted. I can't tell you what the future holds, Domonic. I just want to keep you safe."

I reflected on all that had happened since my uncle's funeral. It all felt so unreal - like I was watching it happen instead of living it. I felt fine. I didn't have any residual anxiety, fear, or trauma. I just felt fine, and that started to make me wonder. Who in their right mind would feel fine about this? Was there something wrong with me?

"Domonic, are you okay?" Carl looked concerned.

I had no idea how long I had been standing there, staring, lost in thought.

"Yeah, no. Right, yeah, I'm okay."

He didn't look convinced.

"Alright. Well, I saw a Thai place down the street. I'm going to go get something to eat. Are you hungry?"

I hadn't been, but the thought of food sent a growl echoing through my gut.

"Yeah, actually. They have a wicked peanut pad thai dish. Please, and thank you."

Carl nodded and stepped out. I went back to unwrapping all the knick-knacks and the lockbox. I was just about finished when I heard a knock at the door. It was Ruth.

"Is Carl here? I was going to go to the bank now."

She had taken the time to do her hair and get dressed up. I had seen her go out to the bank before - this was definitely for Carl.

"He just ran out to get lunch. Should be back pretty quick though."

She nodded. "Ok, I'll come back in a bit." and headed back to her apartment.

I finished unwrapping the rest of the packages. I stood there for a while, waiting for inspiration. I wanted to put this thing together. Eventually, frustrated, I threw up my hands and turned on the news.

"*More rain is coming in tonight, and a fair chance of thundershowers later. We should see a good three inches come down before we get a break in the weather.*"

I had missed the rain here; it was different than east coast rain. It was softer on the west coast. Or at least it felt that way.

Carl came back in a moment later. I could smell peanut pad thai.

"That is a nice little shop." He set the bags down and went to the sink to wash his hands. "There is a hotel just around the corner too. I was thinking I would sleep there."

I looked up from unpacking the food. "Up to you. You're more than welcome to crash here if you want."

He shook his head as he dried his hands. "We've been side-by-side constantly for the last few days. I'm going to get out of your hair after lunch. I'd like to beat the rain. You get some alone time with your cat. Do some catching up with some friends. If you need me or the car, I'll be a block over."

I grinned at him.

"Don't forget, Ruth wants to go to the bank. You'd better walk her over after lunch."

He gave me a wry look then looked over toward the door.

"I like Ruth. She reminds me of my aunt."

I cracked open my pad thai. It looked like heaven in a tin bowl.

"Thanks for lunch, Carl. I hope your aunt doesn't find you as attractive as Ruth does." I said, grinning into my food.

He looked down and rubbed his ear. "Yeah, let's hope not."

~

"Can I have… a double shot of espresso, in a caramel macchiato?" the young man asked.

Nicole nodded and punched in the order. "$5.80," she said.

He fished around in his pockets and pulled out an assortment of coins and singles. He counted out exact change.

"Thank you. What's your name?"

"Caleb." He said expressionlessly, then turned and walked to the waiting area.

Nicole got to work making his drink. A few minutes later he was out the door.

Bzzz Bzzz Bzzz

Her phone went off in her apron pocket. She glanced at it under the counter.

Kyle had sent three texts.

"Nicole! Domonic is back in town. He was wearing a suit and brought some hot chocolate with him"

"I told him where you work too."

"Matt and I are going out for Ramen later if you're hungry!"

She hadn't thought Domonic would come back after he quit the way he did. She had always liked him, ever since they were in school together. Her mind raced. *Should I text him?* She wondered. She looked at her phone as if it knew the answer. Before she could decide, the door opened, and two customers walked up to the counter.

"Hi there, how can I help you?" She put her phone back and walked up to take their orders.

~

"That was amazing. I've had Thai food - in Thailand. This was better. Carl sat back and looked stunned.

I was elated. "Mmm, yeah it is the best."

Carl rubbed his eyes and got up. "Well, I am going to take Ruth to the bank, and then get a room for the night. If you need anything, please call me. Otherwise, I'll be back at 9am."

I nodded and waved as he left. I sat down in my recliner and put my feet up. Coaldust jumped up into my lap. It was nice to be home.

"Oh Coaldust, I'm going to miss you, buddy. I hope you and Ruth have a nice time together."

He curled up on my chest and closed his eyes. It wasn't long until I drifted off too.

~

"Welcome back."

I entered the clearing to see Dionysus sitting alone at the table, eating some grapes.

"Are you missing me yet?"

I sat down across from him. "What do you mean exactly?" My question was clearly biting, he leaned forward and flashed a predatory smile at me.

"You and I, we clearly had a really good time at the casino. You should be grateful. Most people in your shoes would not have had such an easy start to their journey."

I plucked a grape and rolled it around in my hand. "Did you arrange for me to be abducted?" I asked accusingly.

He looked shocked and saddened.

"No, of course not. I would never intentionally bring harm to you."

His response sent chills through me.

"Why? We don't know each other. I don't even know what this is!" I gestured to the fogged area.

"This is a place in your mind, a meeting place, your partition. It will grow as you grow. Here we can speak with you, and access you as needed."

I didn't like the sound of being "accessed as needed".

"I have so many questions. About everything. I-"

"The lockbox." He raised his hand to stop me. "You will find all of your answers in the lockbox."

He was fading. The fog moved in and grew denser.

"I guess I'm waking up now?"

He leaned back, smiling, and fell into the fog.

I woke up with a start. I could hear thunder rumble, and see flashes of lightning popping in the darkness as I blinked and tried to reorient myself. The sound of rain gently waving back and forth on the windows was soothing and familiar.

The lockbox was sitting there on the table. I got up, picking Coaldust up off my lap and setting him back down on the recliner. I walked over to the table.

"I want to know more."

I set upon the pieces. I had an aching need to solve this puzzle. I tried different combinations and various iterations of the puzzle pieces. I tried testing them systematically, making sure I tried every possible permutation. As the hours passed, my neck began to ache, and my mind felt increasingly fatigued. It was mind-numbing and frustrating. The minutes crept by.

Coaldust had finally decided to come to see what I was doing. He walked among the pieces and pawed at some of them. Apparently finding my task uninteresting, he jumped down off the table. I looked down at him with a touch of jealousy. He didn't have the concerns or cares that I did.

"How are you doing, Coaldust?" I reached down to pet him. He purred and rubbed his head into my hand, circling and rubbing against me. I was happy to oblige and give myself a break. He stood on his back legs and stretched upward against my leg.

Suddenly a fleeting thought came to my mind. I saw it! I looked back at the pieces on the table, and there it was! The pieces, they weren't supposed to go into the lockbox one by one. I had to put them together first – I had to build a key. I could stack them, but how to keep them together? I piled the pieces on the table, the realized – I could put the lockbox down on top!

I looked at Coaldust and gave him a couple pats. "Sorry buddy, I think I figured this out." I started working again with a renewed vigor.

I set the pieces on their ends, trying to build something that would fit the lockboxes holes. My first attempt failed. I tried putting them in randomly in an effort to find buttons or levers to press and found nothing. I tried to place all of the pieces that seemed to fit in various places, but I couldn't get them all to go in at the same time. By my fourth attempt, I was able to fill the entire void in the lockbox, but when it went in, it didn't unlock anything. I changed the position of two similar pieces, but now I couldn't get it to fit halfway in. The sixth attempt was very similar to my fourth iteration, I arranged the pieces in a new order, dropped it down and nothing.

"Fuuuuuck."

I dropped my head onto the top of the lockbox in frustration. Everything I tried left out at least two or more pieces. "What am I missing? What am I doing wrong?"

I got up and looked at the other bottles of wine that were given to me at the wake. None had the aged look of the one I had drunk while I was there.

"Time for a break."

I opened a bottle and filled a glass. I didn't know enough about wine to care whether it breathed or not. The first sip was sweet, with hints of fig, and something else I couldn't place.

"That's nice." I looked at the label, and my heart skipped a beat. The logo on the bottle was the same shape as the slot on the bottom of the lockbox. "What the fuck?" I muttered and went to double check. With the bottle in hand, I returned to the table, set the bottle down and upended the lockbox. It was a match.

"Well, Coaldust, do you have any other insights for me?"

He walked to his litter box, apparently done helping me.

I walked away from the table again. There wasn't anything else I could think of to get the puzzle lock to open.

"Right, well if you change your mind, I'll be in the shower..."

I stood in the shower, feeling the comforting warm water run over me, and pondered. I didn't know what to do next. I had no experience with puzzle locks. "Maybe I need a locksmith or someone who solves puzzles for fun." No one came to mind. What I needed was a break from thinking about it. I tried to put it out of my mind, tried to focus on other things - maybe I should try calling my parents. I still hadn't been able to get a hold of them. I thought about where I would live, what I would do with my time now that I didn't have to work. Nothing I tried could distract me for very long. My thoughts kept returning to the puzzle box.

I turned off the shower, grabbed a towel, and went to my luggage for clothes. Opening my suitcase, I saw the big yellow envelope that I had tossed in my bag before we left. It was the packet Eric had driven back to Baltimore for. My mind raced. I hadn't taken more than a cursory glance at the papers inside. I opened the envelope and pulled out the papers. Each one had a strange shape in the middle of it, oblong rectangles with outcroppings and out of place squares. There were also small triangles in each corner. I stared at one of the sheets, noticing that the triangles in the corners were on their sides. I turned the sheet and laid it down, so that the triangles were all pointing up now. I took the rest of the papers to the table and compared them to the bottom of the lockbox. I saw the same triangles on the bottom of the box.

"YES! I didn't need a locksmith! I needed a key!" I couldn't contain my excitement.

I laid out the papers on the table. I matched the corners of the pages to the triangles on the bottom of the box and carefully arranged them.

Each page was very thin, thin enough that I could easily see my finger on the other side. I aligned the sheets and pressed them all down. They made a defined shape. I picked up the puzzle pieces and laid them down one by one. There was only one possible way to build it. At one point, I had to balance two pieces against each other. I was worried they would fall over, but when they were rested against each other, they settled firmly into the recesses of the other pieces.

"I never would have figured that out."

I picked up the lockbox and lowered it carefully over the arrangement.

Click

"Success! Haha! I got in, Coaldust!"

I looked over at Coaldust, who was now busy cleaning himself on the couch. He seemed underwhelmed.

I slowly opened the lid of the box. Inside, I found a collection of books.

"All that for some books?"

Some of the books looked very old, and others seemed new. There were numbers embossed on the spines. I took out the book marked number one. It appeared to be the oldest one. I opened it. The name signed on the front was one of my uncle's. These were his journals.

I settled into my recliner with the box of books beside me.

"I suppose it would make the most sense to read these in order." I started flipping through some entries.

> "**March 20th, 1967.** I have arrived at Litochoro. I will be heading out tomorrow morning to start my mountain hike, and intend to spend a few days. The intensity of the heat only increased during my drive here. Springtime in Greece. Amazing."

> "**March 22nd, 1967.** I found a strange stone amphitheater in the mountains here. It has some overgrowth, but has made a phenomenal campsite! I have been hearing faint echoes of people talking, I can't make out what they're saying. I am going to look around.

Journal, if you don't hear from me then… I was eaten by cannibals!"

"**March 22nd, 1967.** I didn't find anyone, but I did find a really old bottle of what I am guessing is wine. I found it when I fell down near a tremendous tree next to the amphitheater."

"**March 24th, 1967.** I have consumed this magnificent wine! Annnnd… I think it is very strong! I am very drunk. I heard the voice again and I found the owner!... I'll try to remember to write about it in more detail another day!"

"**April 4th, 1967.** Things have changed. The man that I spoke with on the mountainside of Litochoro, the things we spoke of, they are true! Today I was abducted by two thugs. They hit a speed bump and the trunk flew open. I bounced out of the back, I have some nasty scrapes on my ass and legs. I don't know what they wanted. I hope to never find out…."

~

Knock knock knock

I looked at the door. Then at my phone. I'd been reading for hours.

"Come in!"

The door opened, and Carl came in, carrying coffee.

"Hey Domonic, I brought you some coffee. I…"

He paused as his eyes took in the scene. The lockbox sat open beside my chair. Stacks of journals surrounded me in stacks, now sorted into chronological order.

"I see you've figured out the puzzle lock. Your uncle said it would take you months. I guess he was wrong."

I grabbed a tissue and used it as a bookmark, stood up, and stretched.

"Oh yes, coffee. I've been up for a while. Thank you!"

The coffee was very hot, burning the tip of my tongue when I took the first sip. I set it down on the table. It smelled like roasted hazelnuts and made my head tingle with the promise of caffeine.

"So, there were books in the box?" Carl motioned at the journals.

"These are his journals. They start when he was twenty years old, and the last one is dated the week before his death."

Carl looked doubtful, then shrugged. "If you say so. I wasn't with him all the time, but I never saw him write in a journal, or even mention them."

I put a hand on his shoulder and leveled my eyes to his.

"I think my uncle may have kept many things from you. I have been reading through the first book. His journey through life seems to have been very similar to my own, at least when he was young. He describes things that are hard to believe. In his first few weeks as a vessel, someone tried to abduct him too. They were even less successful than my abductors, though. According to his journal, he stabbed one of them in the hand and broke the other's nose before he ran from them."

The surprise on Carls' face was the same expression that had been on mine when I read it. "I'm still reading though. I'll keep pouring over the pages and absorb what I can."

I watched Carl move towards the journals. "Don't let it consume you. You may want to take some notes too. Did you want to go anywhere today?"

I shook my head. "No, I really need to read these. I want to know what's happening to me."

Carl nodded. "If you have any questions, feel free to ask me. Your uncle wanted me to refrain from talking to you until after you'd opened up the lockbox." He sat down on the arm of the couch. "I could maybe fill in a few blanks now."

"What *is* happening to me!?" I was almost shouting. I was wild-eyed, and the need to know was consuming me.

Carl took a deep breath and motioned for me to sit. He took a sip of his coffee.

I sat and listened.

Chapter Eight
New Revelations

"The bloodline of a vessel is ancient, and it goes back farther than any living person can fathom. The unique gift of these bloodlines is that they are capable of containing the raw power of a god. When one of the gods inhabits the body of a vessel, the mortal used to gain access to tremendous power. The god would also have a channel for their power to properly flow into this world."

I nodded as he spoke.

"Your uncle was a vessel, and you are as well. You carry the same blood. The day you were abducted, you were inhabited by a God. He took you for a joy ride to the casino, and you witnessed a small amount of what he can, and will, do with you."

The journals had hinted at this but hadn't outright spoken about being possessed. It referred to the gods as visitors – and I had had no idea they were gods.

"So, I'm a God sock? Just something to wear and walk around in?"

Carl shook his head. "No, they have to come to you first. I don't know how that works. Your uncle never met with anyone, he just got possessed."

"So, that's my life now? Whenever the gods want a joyride, they just come to me? Like some kind of body slave?

"Calm down Domonic. You *are* able to refuse them. I think." Carl said in a placating voice.

I was hopeful that I could just tell them to go away.

He looked at me seriously "There are bigger things to worry about, though."

My face almost jumped off my head. I stood up.

"What do you mean!? I am facing a lifetime of Godly hijackings - and there's worse? Jesus fucking Christ!" I paced across the room; my fists were clenched so hard my knuckles went white. My hands ached. My feet thumped as I walked back and forth through the apartment.

Carl waited.

I didn't know what to do with myself. I paced
back to the chair, but couldn't sit down. The
journals around it seemed to be watching me.

... Jesus f - wait. Carl. Is Jesus....?"

Carl raised his hands.

"I don't know who the gods are. I don't know if
your uncle knew. Yes, you can be taken on a joy
ride." He paused. "BUT - and there is a big *BUT*
- not all Gods just want to drink, fuck, and play
games. Some want to fight, some want to kill,
some want to hunt, some want to learn, and
others want you to die. Your uncle told me that
much about them. He said he had to be careful,
and that was why he hired me, although I never
did have to deal with them."

"What!? Carl! I... I gotta - man." I stumbled
over my words, my mind reeled. I couldn't take
it. "I-I'm going out. I need air. I muttered.

I left. I run-walked down the street. I just
needed to get away, to get my head clear. My
mind was drowning, unable to come up with a
plan or to think of where to go. I went

automatically, wherever my legs took me, and just kept going.

~

"And that's why I came to you. I know I sound insane, and I'm sorry it's so late, but I had to get it all out to someone that wasn't a part of all this, and my feet brought me to your door."

Nicole looked at me with concern. Her face was hard to read. I had told her most of everything I had been through. I rubbed my face in embarrassment. She had been sitting there listening to me for several hours. Nicole stirred her tea and let out a tremendous sigh.

"Dom... I've known you for a long time. This is... way out there. Are you okay?"

I put my head in my hands. "Yeah, I guess." The real answer was no.

She cleared her throat. "Dom, I want you to know that I don't think you're crazy. I just have trouble believing a lot of this."

I pulled out my phone, turned it on, tapped at the screen, and handed it to Nicole. I watched her face.

"Oh my God. That is a lot of money, Dom."

I absently clicked my tongue and bit my pinky. "Yeah… it's a lot."

I put my hand out for the phone. She handed it back.

"If you want to meet Carl, you can. He can confirm it all. You are welcome to look at the journals too. Or you can hang around until I get taken for a joy ride."

She stood and picked up her purse.

"Sure! I would like to meet Carl."

I hadn't expected her to agree. I got up with her, and we started walking back to my place.

"Dionysus, huh?" She said with disbelief. She rubbed her brow, and half laughed. "Maybe the shock of your inheritance has stressed you out too much?"

I nodded fervently. "Yeah, definitely. But it's not the money. Although I haven't even had time to come to grips with the idea of the money yet."

She sighed and rubbed her hand on my back.

"It'll be okay Dom."

~

"No, his phone is shut off. I can't reach him. He's been gone for five hours now. I know he is probably fine, I just don't like not knowing where he is. Wait...."

I could hear Carl through the door as I fumbled with the lock. Finally, my apartment door swung open. I stepped in, followed by Nicole.

"Domonic!" Carl exclaimed. I could clearly hear the relief in his voice. "I was worried! What if something had happened to you, sir?

I flinched at being called "Sir" but let it go.

"Sorry. I just needed some solitude." I motioned to Nicole. "Nicole, this is Carl. Carl, this is Nicole."

Carl raised his eyebrows. "Ohhh, you're Nicole."

She blushed and looked at me.

"Yes, and it is nice to meet you, Carl. Domonic explained to me what he thinks is happening to him, and I thought you could help shed some light on it for me."

Carl looked from her to me. I nodded, and Carl took a seat.

"What do you need to be clarified?"

Carl brought her a chair from the kitchen, and she sat between us.

"I know that he has inherited a huge amount of money. But he said some things about being a vessel. I'd like to know if you can expand on that at all." She left the question open, obviously not wanting to lead him.

Carl looked back at me.

"What have you told her so far? Everything up until today, I imagine."

I nodded, picked up a journal, and started flipping through the pages.

"Dominic inherited both his uncle's fortune, as well as his -occupation - as a vessel for ancient beings known as Gods. This has been passed down through many men in his family's history, and now from his uncle to him."

Nicole's jaw dropped. She guffawed at him. "Really? Just kind of expecting me to accept that?" She looked around the room, her eyes wide with disbelief

Carl shrugged. "Your acceptance or belief is irrelevant. Those are the facts about his life now. If you choose to not believe it, it will not change what he is going to go through for the rest of his life."

My hackles raised as Carl spoke. He hadn't provided me many reasons to weather much more shit today.

She looked at Carl with a menacing expression. I went back to the journal. I was looking for something I read earlier in the day.

"Are *you* doing this to him!? Isn't he going through enough with his uncle dying and having this massive inheritance changing his whole life? Who do you think you are, feeding him these lies!?" Her voice raised up enough to prickle my skin.

Carl leveled his gaze at her. He pulled his shoulders back and raised his chin.

"Mind your tone around Mr. Anth, please! I will be more than happy to continue this conversation in another location if you would like."

But she was on a roll now.

"No, I think he needs to hear everything YOU have to say!"

Carl stood. The movement was smooth and effortless, his body language warning of violence. His mouth opened to retort -

I stood up and marched to the kitchen, taking the journal with me. Carl and Nicole turned to watch me. I opened a drawer and pulled out a paring knife, then returned to the living room. Carl's eyes widened, and Nicole raised her hands.

"Dom?"

I flipped open the journal. I had been holding the page with my thumb. I read clearly and loudly.

"DIONYSUS! INSEWN ONE! INSPIRER OF FRENZIED WOMEN! HEAR ME! A CHANNEL EVOKED UPON MY BODY AND SOUL! A BLOODS SACRED RAGE DELIGHT!"

Carl immediately took a knee and stared at the floor. Nicole stood with her mouth hanging wide. Coaldust hissed, jumped off the kitchen counter, and ran to his cat tree.

I sliced through the skin of my palm.

"Dom!" Nicole cried she ran towards me, but only made it a few steps before being forced back by a wave of energy.

My vision changed. The room was awash in a faint glow, like an overexposed photo. My entire body was humming with energy. My skin felt like it was prickling with needles. I returned to the journal page.

"RISE NOW! I WELCOME YOU! RETURN TO THIS COIL AND JOIN WITH ME!

I thrust my hand above my head and clenched my fist tight. Blood dripped down into my mouth. I dropped the paring knife on the ground.

Nicole stared as the cut on my hand healed before her eyes. A bottle of water on the table turned dark red, and the faint glow brightened for a brief moment as energy poured from me, the lights brightened and the crackle of electricity coursed through the bulbs. The room went completely dark for a moment before the lights came back on.

We stood before Nicole. Her eyes looked back at us, wide and confused. She dropped into a chair.

"Dom?"

"That's her, we've known each other for years. I know this isn't what you probably had in mind for your next visit, but she needs to understand the truth." I thought to Dionysus.

We saw Carl kneeling.

"Carl, get up my friend. You do not kneel to me." His voice was powerful, different from the first time he had taken over.

"Dionysus?"

We looked at Nicole. She was gripping the seat so tightly that her knuckles were white.

"Yes, I am Dionysus. Domonic is here as well. We both hear you. He tells me you need proof of his new life."

We motioned to the bottle on the table, and it moved towards Nicole.

"Drink."

Nicole hesitantly opened the bottle, sniffed it suspiciously, and took a tentative sip. It was red wine - smooth, sweet, and full-bodied. She coughed, apparently not prepared for the taste. She stared at the bottle in her hand.

Carl stood and extended his hand. "Dionysus, I didn't think you answered a summons."

We shook his hand. "I don't normally, though I do like this vessel. I thought it prudent to help him… for now."

Nicole stood, her knees shaking. She walked toward us.

"You're a God?" She reached out and touched my arm, then reflexively pulled away as if she'd been shocked.

"Yes. I am Dionysus! Now, you can accept what he has told you, or you can run away. There is no point in remaining in his life if you doubt what he is." We motioned to the door. It flung open, then slammed shut. She jumped and cried out, startled.

"No! I'll stay! I believe!"

We looked to Carl, then back to Nicole.

"*Thank you, Dionysus.*" I thought.

"*Don't worry about it; I told you I would be gentle.*"

Nicole sat down and stared at us. "What happens now?"

Carl sat as well. "He will do as he wishes. I may be summoned to follow and keep him safe. If not, Domonic will be returned to us when Dionysus is finished." We looked at Nicole and gave her a soft smile.

"I won't stay long. I came to answer a plea, and I believe my purpose is served. Farewell for now, Carl. Next time we're going out drinking and we'll find some women together."

Carl laughed and bowed his head. "Yes, my lord."

We sat in the recliner. A flash of light raced over the room, and then everything faded to darkness.

~

"He's unconscious. He'll probably be out until morning" Carl explained. "Nicole, we can't get angry around him. If he gets too anxious or upset, he could accidentally let in a god that he doesn't want. It could invite chaos, pain, suffering, or death to him, or anyone around him."

She looked uneasy. "What can I do to help?"

Carl slumped into the couch and threw his arms wide. "That is a question I can't answer. His uncle always kept away from people he might have loved. He didn't maintain any close relationships. He treated this like an obligation, a duty. I doubt that Domonic will treat it the same way."

She sat back and looked between us blankly. After a moment she managed to speak. "How long does he have to live like he's on happy pills?" She had tears in her eyes. "Carl, is he going to be okay?" Her voice cracked, and the tears rolled down her cheeks.

"His uncle lived a full and adventurous life. He died of natural causes, after many decades of being a vessel. I would assume the same possibility exists for Domonic."

She looked hopeful. "Would it be okay if I stayed with him for a while?" She placed a hand on Domonic's arm. He sighed at the touch but did not wake.

Carl raised an eyebrow. "I think that would be good for him. At least for a while. Eventually, he will learn how to control the channels that lead into him, and no God will be able to jump in uninvited."

Carl got up and retrieved a blanket from the bedroom. He covered Domonic, then went and laid down on the couch. "The bed is yours if you want it. Domonic will rise with the sun, and so will I."

Nicole set the bottle on the table and walked towards the bedroom. "Thank you, Carl."

He shook his head at her. "If he wants you to leave, you leave. No questions." Nicole nodded and started walking towards the bedroom again.

"Nicole, I'm sorry for how I spoke to you earlier. My first duty is to keep Domonic safe. I shouldn't have treated you like that."

Nicole slowly nodded. "I think I understand. Let's just focus on Dom."

Carl bowed his head and closed his eyes, taking a deep breath, and not inviting further conversation.

Nicole walked into the bedroom and laid down. She hadn't been in Domonic's room in months. They had never really had a formal relationship. They had tried a couple of times to start something, but life always seemed to get in the way. She was afraid for him, and she didn't like that this Carl seemed to think he had the right to get between them. Tears ran down her face. Was she going to lose him to Carl and these gods?

"Good night Dom, I hope your dreams are peaceful." she whispered.

~

"Not bad, if I do say so myself!" Dionysus sat at the table in the partition.

"She definitely believes what I told her now." I sat across from Dionysus and took a deep breath. "How did my uncle do this for most of his life?"

His sigh was deep and empathetic. "My little mortal friend, your uncle was very picky about who could utilize him as a vessel. I saw his journals in your apartment. You need to read them and get to know your uncle. Most of my family loves vessels, but there are some that are not as fond of them. Just be careful, and try to live with positive emotions. Negative ones will let the dark beings in. If they get control of you, they will not let go easily."

His words eased me tremendously. I let out a deep breath. Knowing that I had some measure of control over dark beings getting inside of me was a relief.

"Thank you, Dionysus. I should get some sleep now."

Dionysus stood and walked into the fog. His words echoed as he faded.

"You should work on your partition. This is where you're going to spend most of your time when one of us borrows your body. It's boring right now."

~

Birds were chirping gently outside as the last drops of rain trickled from the sky. The sun crested the horizon and light warmed the room. I opened my eyes and could smell coffee.

"Good morning. That was quite the display last night, Domonic." Carl said from the kitchen. He was pouring a cup of coffee. "Are you alright?"

I sat up and inspected myself, squeezing the hand that I had cut. "I think so; I thought I had cut my hand…?"

Carl approached and set two cups of coffee down on the table with one hand, and held another in his other hand for himself.

"You did. Some Gods will help you with healing things like that. One time, I watched your uncle get into a bar fight with a dozen men because a God asked him to."

My eyes shot wide. I couldn't imagine my uncle getting in a fight, let alone with a dozen men.

"Which God was riding him then?" I asked hoping to know which one to avoid.

"He was not possessed at the time, though he did do as he was asked. I was told not to interfere. I watched your uncle take a beating that should have killed him." Carl paused. He stared past me, remembering the incident. "After I got him into the car, the God that had asked him to do it jumped in, healed him, and then went back into the bar and beat those men to the edge of death." Carl took a long slow sip of his coffee.

"I don't want to do that." I shook my head and started blowing at my coffee.

Nicole came out of the bedroom wrapped in a blanket.

"Good. I don't want you beaten to death either."

I pressed the coffee cup to my lips. We sat in silence, sipping our coffees. Carl finished his and moved over to the couch next to me. He spoke softly.

"I'm going to go back to my hotel to shower and change. I'll be back in a little while. Nicole wants to talk to you about something important. Try to hear her out." He stood and gave a casual wave to the two of them.

"See you soon. Talk with him about it." And he left.

"Nicole?" I kept my coffee near my face. It felt safer hiding behind the cup.

She moved down the couch and sat near the recliner. "Last night was fucking crazy. If I hadn't been here to see it, I wouldn't believe it." She put her coffee down and pulled the blanket tight around her. "I asked Carl what I could do to help you, help keep you safe. He said your uncle didn't have anyone like me, just him."

I stopped drinking my coffee and listened. It was a relief to be able to talk with someone that knew about what I was going through.

"Dom, I want to be here for you, with you. I want to help you."

It was sudden and unexpected. I felt my shoulders heave. I dropped the cup as the tears erupted and I started to sob uncontrollably. Nicole was instantly beside me, holding me, wrapping her blanket around us both.

"It is okay, Dom. I'm here."

Even in the comfort of her arms, the reality of the dangers I had faced fell down around me. I was filled with terror of what the future held. I felt myself be pulled down into the murky darkness of these thoughts and feelings.

"HELLO LITTLE VESSEL!"

The voice felt like cold mucus running down my throat. I panicked and tried to retreat from it. I could no longer see my living room. I focused on the table in the fog in my partition and ran.

"RUN ALL YOU WANT, DOMONIC! I'M COMING FOR YOU!"

"Dom! Snap out of it!" I could hear Nicole's voice, faint and far away. The partition shook back and forth like it had when I was with

Dionysus, when Carl had shaken me awake. This fog wasn't fading though.

"Who are you?" I called out as I ran through the fog.

"I AM THE DARKNESS. I AM CHAOS! I AM EREBUS! AND TOGETHER WE SHALL BE A MAELSTROM OF PANDEMONIUM AND FEAR UPON THE WORLD!"

I ran fast and hard, but it was like running in Jello. Tendrils of shadow reached out and caressed my neck. I felt myself slowing down. I pushed harder, panicked. I could see the table coming into my sight. I kept moving towards it, but then it wasn't me moving anymore.

"Dom! Please!" Her voice strained and broke. She gasped as I blinked and stood up, looking down at her.

"HELLO THERE, LITTLE HUMAN"

Nicole backed away slowly. Those terrible eyes - my eyes, but not my eyes - followed her.

"Who are you?"

I could feel the jagged and unnatural smile. My lips stretched uncomfortably.

"I AM THE DARKNESS. I AM CHAOS. I AM EREBUS! COME HERE LITTLE ONE. I MUST KNOW YOU."

I was crawling through the fog, and the darkness was pulling me back so hard that it was difficult to move forward at all. I could see Nicole's frightened face, my apartment superimposed in my vision.

"Hang on Nicole, I'm almost there!" I yelled.

But my lips didn't form the words. Instead, they grinned that evil grin.

Nicole was cornered. I reached for her, and this time my hand extended toward hers.

"GIVE ME YOUR HAND, LITTLE ONE."

Erebus grinned and hummed as she complied. He gently stroked her hand with his thumb and lifted it to my face. I could feel her hand trembling in mine, and see her face wince at the touch. Reflected in her eyes, I could see the evil grin on my face spread to a thin smile. My eyes narrowed, and a bead of red light flared in them.

"P-please…" Nicole stammered.

"PLEASE? HOW POLITE OF YOU TO ASK!"

My mouth shot open, but it was not my mouth. My lips stretched and parted, tearing in places as they revealed a mouth full of needle-like fangs. Erebus clamped onto Nicole's hand, sucking her blood into his mouth. I could taste the warm, salty, metallic flavor. The bite was so fast, Nicole hadn't even flinched before he released her. Now, I could see the expression on her face as her body registered the pain.

Erebus looked at her and seemed dazed himself.

"WELL, THAT IS DELICIOUSLY UNEXPECTED!" He looked down at her and let go of her hand. She pulled it to her chest protectively. "WHAT IS YOUR NAME, LITTLE ONE?"

I was horrified. What did he have in store for her? I renewed my focus on breaking free.

"Just... a little... farther!" I was pulling with everything I had in me. I screamed. Bloody saliva ran from my mouth, sweat ran down my face and dripped off my chin. I pulled, inch by inch, as the table drew nearer, and the darkness slowly retreated, until finally I had made it back into the partition. The darkness faded as it became easier to pull myself the rest of the way.

"FINE!! IF YOU DON'T WANT TO ANSWER ME, YOU LITTLE BITCH, I'LL RIP THE ANSWERS FROM YOUR SKULL!" Erebus screamed. He lifted my hands. I could feel intense pain as my nails elongated into long, sharp points. He lunged forward at Nicole- and fell to the ground.

I vomited and thrashed on the floor. It felt like there were ice picks under my fingernails. My head spun with pain and vertigo, and my body seized uncontrollably.

Suddenly, Carl was kneeling beside me.

"Domonic!" He shouted, and that was the last I knew as the world faded to darkness.

~

Carl quickly set to work stabilizing Domonic. He grabbed a couch cushion and gently lifted his head on top of it. His body was still shaking, but it was getting better. Finally, he lay still, breathing the slow deep breaths of sleep.

With Domonic apparently stable, Carl turned to Nicole.

"Nicole, are you alright?"

She couldn't answer. She held out her damaged hand to Carl.

He frowned. "I'll be right back. I have a first aid kit in the car."

Carl came back with a gray hard-shell case. He opened it to reveal a very extensive first aid kit. He donned a pair of nitrile gloves, then gently sterilized her hand. She bit her lip and furrowed her brow at the pain. Gently and carefully, Carl applied a topical antibiotic ointment before wrapping it lightly with gauze. He taped down the end of the gauze and wrapped her hand in a compression bandage.

"We'll need to check on it later to make sure it's not infected. You might need to go to the hospital." She absently nodded, tears running silently down her face. Her eyes were fixed on Domonic with a mixture of worry and fear.

Carl set about cleaning up the mess. "He will be alright, you know. Do you know who was in him?"

She looked up at Carl "E- Erebus?"

Carl froze. Fear drew onto his face.

"That's not good." He sat against the wall. "His uncle once told me that if Erebus ever took over his body, I was to shoot him dead before he could do something awful. I don't know how Domonic managed to stop him. I'm glad he did though."

Nicole gently rubbed at the bandage on her hand. "Thank you, Carl. I think I need to lay down." Her face showed fatigue. She had a distant look in her eyes. She walked back into the bedroom, dragging the blanket behind her.

Carl pulled out his phone and typed an email to Mr. Donovan. "Your uncle was never this exciting, Domonic." He put his phone away and finished cleaning. Then, he carefully lifted Domonic and carried him to the couch. He tucked the cushion back under his head and draped a blanket over him.

Carl peeked in at Nicole. She had fallen asleep on the bed. Quietly, he packed up the first aid kit and headed down to return it to the car. On his way back up, his phone rang, it was Mr. Donovan.

"Hello?"

"CARL!" Carl quickly pulled the phone away from his ear. "CARL, EREBUS SHOWED UP?! THE LAST TIME HE CAME AROUND I SPENT NEARLY TWO YEARS OF MY LIFE WORKING TO GET MICHELLE OUT OF PRISON! HE WAS WANTED IN THREE COUNTRIES, CARL, THREE! DO YOU HAVE ANY IDEA WHAT THAT THING IS CAPABLE OF!?" Eric sounded terrified. He was breathing heavily over the phone, incoherent muttering leaked through the earpiece. "Listen to me Carl: I am almost at Seattle. I told Domonic I'd be there at the end of the month. I didn't think he'd be having visitors so damn soon. Keep that boy calm until I get there!"

"Yes, sir. Domonic is very lucky to have not hurt anyone too badly. The situation is contained now, Erebus is no longer in control of him. I will let you know if anything else happens. Was there anything else?"

Mr. Donovan's breath shuddered on the other end. "No, I suppose not. Just keep him safe until he gets a good hold of this thing. We can't have some God of murder or something taking over and going on a rampage."

Carl stopped halfway up to the apartment. "I understand. I will do anything I can to keep him safe. I do have to get back to him now though. We'll talk again soon." Carl hung up before Mr. Donovan could say anything else and returned to the apartment. He sat and watched Domonic for a good long while.

Chapter Nine
Indeterminate Futures

"This is what happens if he gives in to negative emotions?"

Nicole had taken a shower and was wearing her clothes from the night before.

Carl gestured to the journals. "The answers are probably in there, although he is the only one who is supposed to read them." He replied, pointing at Domonic, still unconscious on the couch.

"Well, I'm going to keep him happy then. We have a mutual friend - Kyle. He's always telling me how much Domonic likes me." She blushed and fidgeted her fingers nervously. "You know, the first time he asked me out on a date, I said yes. I was so excited, but it never happened. My sister turned up at my door and ended up staying with me. Her boyfriend had started hitting her, and she needed me. The second time he asked me out, I was all ready to go when his neighbor Ruth fell and broke her hip."

"I've met Ruth, she's very sweet." Carl replied.

"Anyway, that second date didn't happen, and then Dom was busy with helping Ruth until she got back on her feet again. The third time, we agreed to just have coffee at work as our first date. We did, and it was nice. We had been friends for a long time by then…" She wiped away tears from her cheeks. "Can you help move him to the bed?" I think he'd sleep better there.

Carl gently picked up Domonic and easily carried him to the bed.

"Thank you," said Nicole. Carl nodded and left the room. She crawled in next to him and tucked the covers around them both. "Dom, if you can hear me… I'm here. I'm not leaving. I promise."

~

I looked around and grinned, pleased with myself. "That's better! We'll see what Dionysus thinks of my partition next time he comes around."

Pleased as I was, my shoulders still sagged. I was tired from the effort. What had once been a small garden area, with a dining table and chairs, was now a large grove. Trees lined the

229

perimeter, keeping the fog restrained on the other side. A small brook wound through the grove, with delicate water plants growing at the edges and water lilies floating in a small connected pond. In the centre was a large gazebo, with a table and chairs to seat a dozen people. Lounging chairs with umbrellas and small side tables were strategically placed, a few in such a way that you could sit with your feet in the brook.

One chair at the table stood out from the rest. It was made of stone that I had pulled up from the ground. Early in the reconstruction, Dionysus had explained how my intent and will would help to manifest things in this place. The chair was designed with the intent that only I could sit in it. If Erebus, or any other unwelcome god ever took control of me again, all I would have to do is sit in my special chair, and it would eject them from my body. Next to the stone chair was a small silver bell, like a doorbell to my partition. If a God wanted to speak to me, they need only ring the bell.

"Dom, if you can hear me... I'm here and I'm not leaving. I promise." I could hear her voice, distant and warm, whispering in the brook.

I felt the fog strain against the trees. It was trying to take me from the partition, but the trees held firm. It was time to return though. I walked to the stone chair and sat down. I closed my eyes and relaxed, and imagined waking up.

~

I opened my eyes. Nicole was asleep next to me. I moved gingerly and slid out of the bed. With a glance back to make sure I hadn't woken her, I quietly left the room. The journals were now arranged in a neat pile on the table beside my chair. Candles, a notepad, and some pens were gathered on the side table. Carl was on the couch.

"Hey, Carl. Everything okay?" I asked as I closed the bedroom door.

He nodded. "Yes, I think so. Are *you* alright sir?" He spoke softly.

There was an uncomfortable silence.

"I have no choice, do I? I either embrace this, or I risk hurting more people." I walked into the kitchen and found a bottle of wine. I opened a bottle of wine and tried rinsing my mouth out. It did nothing but burn my cracked lips. I spit the wine out in the sink. "I can taste her blood still. I hate this."

Carl walked over with a flask in hand. "Try this. It'll strip the taste from your mouth."

I swished the drink around in my mouth. The vapors burned my eyes and lips, bringing tears to my eyes. I spat it into the sink.

"Gaaah! What is that?"

Carl chuckled and closed the flask. "Grain alcohol. It has many uses."

I reeled slightly and made my way to my chair. It was difficult to not cough.

"Well, thank you. I appreciate it. I'm going to read these journals. Hopefully once I'm done, I'll be able to figure out what to do with myself."

Carl put a hand on my shoulder. "Alright, I'm going to go get some more supplies. You need groceries too. I'll be back." He left, closing the door softly.

I sat down and opened the journal to where I had left off. I was instantly captivated.

~

"I wish you wouldn't antagonize him. He's still new to this. And the others haven't had a chance to make use of him yet."

"HAHAHA!!! JUST A LITTLE FUN! HIS FRIEND IS CERTAINLY DELICIOUS. I WOULD LIKE TO EAT HER!" His laughter was like nails on a chalkboard. It ruined the serenity of the vineyard.

Dionysus sighed as he inspected his grapes. "Oh, dear Erebus, you do like to tempt chance, don't you?"

Erebus paused and thought sincerely about it. "NO MORE THAN ANYONE ELSE. I THINK YOU WOULD BE INTERESTED IN HER TOO. I DID LEAVE A LITTLE SOMETHING WITH HER!"

"Erebus! What do you mean -".Dionysus stood up and turned toward him, but he was gone. "Oh, never mind."

He had other things to think on. "Grow my little luscious gems. Grow and ready yourselves. You are going to make a wonderful vintage!"

~

Nicole shot out of bed when she woke to find Domonic missing. She looked around the room carefully, not knowing if Dom or some evil god might be standing in the corner, but she was alone in the room. She cracked open the door and could see Domonic sitting in his favorite chair, reading a journal. Carl was not in the room. She quietly moved out to the couch and sat down, watching him, he didn't look up. She didn't think he realized she was there. She didn't interrupt him, she sat and watched him read.

After about an hour, Carl came back. Domonic didn't even look up, didn't seem disturbed at all. Carl was carrying several bags of groceries and a backpack. He put the groceries away, then motioned for Nicole to step outside with him.

"Do you own your home?" Nicole nodded.

"Great, we'll head there. You'll need to pack if you're coming with us. When he's done with the journals, he will want to travel. The journals will likely talk about some of the places his uncle would want him to go."

Nicole sat up straight and took a deep breath. She realized she would have to make a choice and would have to make it now if she wanted a life with Domonic.

She looked at Carl and nodded slowly.

"Right. With everything that's happened, I almost forgot that he is fabulously wealthy now. He doesn't need to stay in one place." *and if I don't go with him, I can't expect he'll come back to me.* "Let's go. Is this your car?"

Carl nodded.

"Ooooh! Can I ride in the back? It looks super comfy!"

Carl opened the door for her. "Absolutely, Domonic prefers to ride up front. I'm not used to that."

She got in, giggled and buckled herself in. "I'm like one of those rich ladies in the movies, sitting back here. All I need is a fur coat!" She tried to lighten the mood.

"Alright, where am I going?" Carl asked, not amused.

Nicole gave him directions to her apartment. It was less than 5 minutes away. They both went up, and Carl helped her clean out her fridge and pack her luggage. As she packed, Nicole tried to focus her mind on all the future possibilities, for travel and adventure. With Domonic.

"Nicole, do you know how to use a taser?" Carl asked, reaching into his backpack.

The unexpected question brought Nicole back from her daydreaming. Her smile faded.

"No… I've never used one."

Carl pulled out a small brown box.

"Even with a God inhabiting him, his body is still human. If you zap him with this, it will drop him the same as anyone else. Keep it on you, and use it if you need to."

She took the box from Carl and opened it. Inside was a jet black taser. She picked it up and looked at it.

"All you have to do is squeeze it and push."

She squeezed it, and the taser turned on. It crackled and popped violently. She loosened her grip and tried it again. She thought of the way Dom's body had morphed when Erebus had possessed him. The inhuman grin with devil's teeth that so easily pierced her skin, and the long sword-tip nails. She rubbed her hand, feeling the pain of the bite. Was he really still just a fragile human?

Carl could see the doubt on her face.

"Thank you, Carl, I appreciate it." Nicole tucked the taser into her purse and returned to packing. When she was sure she had everything she needed, she made three phone calls. The first was to her bank to set all her bills on autopay. The second, to her parents, telling them she was going traveling with Domonic. They were happy that the two of them had finally gotten together. It was hard to get off that call - her mom wanted all the details of where they were going and how long they'd be gone. She finally came up with a story that Dom was surprising her with a trip, and she didn't know where. That got her mom even more excited, but at least she stopped asking for details. The third call was to the coffee shop where she worked. She told her boss she had to quit - a once in a lifetime opportunity had presented itself, and she couldn't turn it down. She wasn't very impressed with not getting two weeks' notice and having shifts to cover. Nicole felt terrible about it, but it was something she had to do. Now she understood what Dom had had to do when he had to call and quit on Kyle.

She took a deep breath. "Alright, Carl I am ready."

He picked up her luggage and carried it down for her. They got back in the car and drove back to Domonic's in silence.

~

The hesitant knock at the door broke my concentration.

"Yes, one moment!" I called. I placed a bookmark in the journal and went to the door. It was Ruth.

"Dommy? Are you okay? There have been some weird noises coming from your apartment since you and your friend came back." Her face was heavy with concern. She was a little old angel.

238

"Oh yeah, sorry about that. We just got carried away with the - uh - movie."

She nodded, then peered past me.

"Did you want me to take Coaldust now?"

Coaldust ran out from his cat tree and ran to Ruth, rubbing against her legs in greeting.

"Yeah, I think he's ready for you now. I'll drop off the rest of his stuff in just a little while. Thank you again, Ruth."

She cupped my cheek in her hand.

"You be careful out there Dommy. The world is bigger than you might think."

I reached up and took her hand in mine.

"You be careful too, Ruth. I'll check in from time to time."

She shook her head and chuckled. "You don't worry about me now. Thanks to you, Coaldust and I might even take a trip on a train soon."

Tears crept into the corners of my eyes. "That sounds really nice, Ruth. You and Coaldust have a good time."

"Come on, Coaldust." She squeezed my hand, turned, and walked back to her apartment. Coaldust followed on her heels.

"Goodbye Coaldust." I said to the empty hallway.

I returned to the journals, ready to move forward. I had just sat down when the door opened and Nicole walked in with Carl. They were both carrying luggage. I looked at them with confusion.

"Nicole? I thought you were sleeping." I looked from the bedroom back to her. She smiled and rolled her eyes.

I melted. I loved that familiar smile, the one she had when she was amused at some stupid thing I said or did. My eyes lingered on her. I hadn't felt this way in a long time and hadn't realized how much I had missed her.

"I uh… right. I have something to do somewhere I'm sure." Carl muttered lamely. He set the suitcase down and left the apartment.

Nicole held my gaze, and our eyes explored each other. The room felt completely empty except for the two of us. I got up out of my chair, stumbling over the pile of journals. I recovered myself and walked toward her carefully, afraid to scare her. I felt a pang of guilt as I noticed the bandaging on her hand.

"Nicole…" I said softly. "It's me, Nicole.

She bit her bottom lip. Her purse fell to the floor. "Dom?" She folded her arms in front of herself protectively. I closed the distance between us and embraced her in a tender hug. She leaned her head on my chest, and we stood there for several minutes. Eventually she pulled back to look up at me, and I leaned forward to kiss the top of her forehead.

"I am so sorry I hurt you."

She pushed me to arm's length. I knew this face too.

"Dom, stop. That was not you! We both know it. Listen to me. I just quit my job, threw out all my food, and put all my bills on autopay. I'm not running away *from* you, from this." She pointed at me and then her hand. "I'm running away *with* you." It was a statement, not a question. "I even called my parents and told them you and I were seeing each other."

I was taken aback by how forward she was being. She was almost aggressive. Maybe I should have been put off by her assuming she was invited, but I wasn't.

"You told your parents that we are…"

She nodded. "Yeah, I told them we'd finally started seeing each other."

She stood on her toes, pulled me in, and kissed me as if sealing the deal. She pulled away and grinned up at me. "You know, I figure since we're together, we might as well… be together." This time it was a question - an invitation. Her grin reached her eyes, which held salacious promises in them.

"Wow. Nicole. I-I…" I stumbled over my words, and a flush crept up my neck.

"'Wow' is exactly what I was thinking." She grabbed my hand and pulled me toward the bedroom. I followed obediently, kicking the door closed behind us.

~

Carl was waiting in line. His stomach growled, and his mouth watered at the smell of the pad thai wafting through the air. The lady taking orders cleared the customer in front of him and waved him forward, smiling.

"Next!"

Carl walked up and flashed a smile back at her. "Hello, I would love two orders of your peanut pad thai, please."

She punched the order into her till. "That's $27.98."

Carl handed her two twenty dollar bills. "Keep the change."

She nodded and motioned for him to move to the side. A few minutes later his order came up in a to-go bag.

"Double order, peanut pad thai!"

Carl raised his hand and eagerly took the bag. "Thank you."

He walked out of the shop and leisurely headed back to the apartment, taking his time. He walked down the hall and stopped at the door to Ruth's apartment. He knocked and could hear movement inside. Ruth opened the door and looked at him with a surprised smile.

"Hello there, Carl. Can I help you?"

He lifted the bag. "Would you like some lunch? It's peanut pad thai."

She looked over her shoulder and then back to him. "Oh! Yes, thank you, just -" she paused. "Give me one minute."

She closed the door and hurried to the living room, tidying a few things off the table. Then she headed to the bathroom and checked herself out in the mirror. She quickly brushed her hair, pinched her cheeks, and fluffed out her skirt. "You'll do, Ruth." She said to herself, then returned to the door and opened it wide.

"Please come in."

Carl stepped in and started unpacking the food onto the table.

"Why aren't you having lunch with Dommy?" She asked curiously.

"Oh, well, I stepped out to give him and Nicole some privacy."

With surprising speed, she took a seat. "He is alone with a girl over there? Oh good! I have been hoping he would find a nice young lady to take care of him."

Carl chuckled and looked at Ruth. "I got this from the Thai place down the street, have you tried it before?"

She raised an eyebrow at him.

"Right, Domonic probably foisted it onto you at some point."

She leaned back and scoffed at him. "I introduced him to it, just so you know."

Carl sat down looking impressed. "Well Ruth, thank you for the delicious pad thai, and of course the fine company to dine with."

They dug in, humming with appreciation at the delicious food. They chatted idly about the weather and other inconsequential things as they

245

ate. When they were finished, they both leaned back in their chairs.

Ruth looked at Carl mischievously. "So, is this where you swipe the table clean and make ravenous love to me?"

Carl's mouth dropped, and his eyes popped open. He caught a glimpse of the smirk that she was trying to hide. He closed his mouth, focused, and put on the most seductive look he could manage.

"I suppose it is…" He stood up slowly and started meticulously clearing the table. When he heard her laugh, he turned back to look at her. She had a hand over her mouth and was doing a poor job of hiding her amusement. Carl laughed with her.

"Ruth, thank you for lunch."

She walked up to him and squeezed his arm. She could feel the strength in the muscle of his forearm.

"I should be the one thanking you, Carl. Other than Dommy, not many people take the time to visit me, let alone bring me lunch."

Carl brought her in for a hug. "Well everyone else is missing out."

She motioned to the door, and he headed toward it "You get going. I want to have a shower, and you're only welcome to stay if you join me."

He turned to her. "Don't tempt me, Ruth, I have work to do!"

They both laughed as he left.

~

"What did you mean when you said you left a little something with her?"

Erebus smiled and fell to the ground, stretching like a cat. "I BIT HER! SHE HAS THE EREBUS VIRUS NOW. IT SHOULD TAKE HOLD SOON!"

Dionysus had heard of this virus before. It was guaranteed death to a mortal. Their medicine couldn't stop it.

"Is there any particular reason you chose to torment her with certain death?"

Erebus cackled, rolling on the ground. When he finally stopped, he floated back up to his feet, grinning at Dionysus.

"WELL, YOUNG ONE, THAT IS FOR ME TO KNOW, AND ME TO LAUGH ABOUT!"

He vanished in a snap of light. Mouths erupted from below his skin and clothing, all of them laughing in different ways. The mouths fell away leaving no trace of Erebus. The lips, teeth, and tongues he left behind continued to writhe, laughing where he had stood.

"Oh, that is obscene. Away with you now." Dionysus snapped his fingers, and the mouths vanished in a thin cloud of smoke.

~

"I can't believe we waited so long to do this," Nicole said as she rolled over and ran her fingers along my shoulder.

"I am choosing to believe the universe wanted us to wait until now. It feels right to me."

A titter escaped her mouth as she rolled up onto her elbow. "I guess you are probably right. I mean, you are kind of connected to the universe now, aren't you?"

I thought about it and shrugged at her. I had no idea if she was right or not. We both laughed.

"I don't know. It doesn't matter I guess." I leaned my head down to kiss her, she lifted her head and returned the kiss with a subdued vigor.

We were interrupted by the sound of the front door opening.

"Hello!?" Carl called loudly.

"We'll be right out Carl!" I responded.

I turned back to Nicole. My face fell at the look on hers. She was shaking. Thin, light colored blood had started leaking from her eyes, nose, mouth, and ears. Red dots were appearing on her skin, popping up as I watched.

"CARL! HELP!"

Carl kicked the door open. He looked from me to Nicole, and his eyes shot wide.

"Run, Domonic. Go to the car, get the first aid kit from the trunk. RUN!"

I jumped out of bed, ran past Carl, scooping his keys off the table. I fled to the car, barely noticing I was naked as the cool air touched my skin. I grabbed the kit and ran back into the building, sprinted up the stairs and burst back into the bedroom. I put the first aid kit on the bed next to Nicole and tore it open. The blankets and cover sheets were thrown to the side.

"Nicole!"

She didn't respond. I looked at Carl, waiting for him to do something or give me some instruction. He looked at me with utter helplessness.

"I don't know what this is. I can't help her."

Chapter Ten
Choices

Nicole was still shaking. Her breathing got weak and erratic as she gasped and struggled for air. The mottled red rash spread across her delicate skin, and her bandaged hand had started to soak through.

"911 - What is the nature of your emergency?"

"I have a young woman bleeding from her eyes, ears, and mouth. She has red splotches appearing on her skin and is having difficulty breathing."

Carl walked out of the room with the phone. I couldn't hear the rest of what he was saying.

"Is this what's supposed to happen? Huh, Universe?" I asked aloud.

Carl came back into the room. He knelt on the bed and pressed his fingers to the side of her throat. He reached into the first aid kit and pulled out a pad of paper. I watched him write down the time and her pulse reading.

"You should put some clothes on. An ambulance is coming, and I expect you'll want to go with her."

I looked at him dumbly, then looked down, realizing I was still naked. I scrambled to gather my clothes from around the room and dressed hurriedly, keeping my eyes on Nicole the whole time.

A few minutes later, Carl let the paramedics into the room. They were wearing gloves and pushing a stretcher between them. The first, a woman, approached Nicole and shook her roughly by her shoulder.

"Ma'am! Ma'am, can you hear me?"

Nicole made no response. Just the wheezing of her breath.

The paramedic pulled the covers down and rubbed her knuckles roughly against Nicole's sternum.

"Ma'am, can you hear me, ma'am?"

She responded with a weak groan, her eyelids fluttering. A dark bruise formed on her chest in a line down her sternum.

The paramedic gave her partner a meaningful look. With the speed and unison of experience, they wheeled the stretcher next to the bed, tossed off the blankets, and at the count of three, lifted Nicole onto the stretcher.

"We're taking her to Seattle General."

Carl held the door open for them, then came back to me.

I watched them all in a daze.

"Get your shoes on. We're following them. Go now."

"Right, yes. We have to follow them."

I grabbed my jacket and shoved my feet into my shoes, then Carl and I ran out the door. We followed the ambulance directly to the hospital. Carl drove up to the main emergency entrance.

"You go. I'll park and meet you."

I dashed through the doors. I could see the paramedics unloading Nicole from the ambulance through a window. I looked around for someone to help me. The front desk was empty.

Finally, a nurse in a gown and gloves came up to me.

"You came with the girl in the ambulance?"

I nodded, my eyes darting around as I looked for an indication of where Nicole might be.

"Come with me."

She led me into in to the entryway of a hospital room and handed me a gown.

"Put this on."

As I tried to figure out the gown ties, Carl appeared beside me, led by another nurse. He was handed his own gown and had donned it before I had figured out my ties.

The nurse opened the second door leading to Nicole's room and directed us to the corner of the room. A whole team of doctors and nurses circled around Nicole, inserting IV's, drawing blood, and placing a mask on her face. I could guess who the lead doctor was as he was calling out instructions and medical orders I didn't understand. I leaned over to Carl.

"She's not going to make it is she?" My voice broke, and I fought back the tears.

Carl's eyes didn't leave Nicole. "I have seen too many things happen, that should never have happened, while working for your uncle. I can't say she won't make it. I really don't know."

I tried to calm myself. I tried to go to Nicole, to comfort her, but one of the nurses pushed me back gently.

"Please, stay here. We need space to help your friend".

An hour went by, and no one had spoken to us. The frenzy started to die down. Fluid bags of various colours and sizes were hanging on IV poles with lines draped from them. Nicole didn't seem any better. Only one nurse remained, checking her monitors and tubes and writing away on a clipboard. Carl was sitting patiently in a chair. I went to Nicole again, and the nurse didn't stop me. I stood there, gently holding her good hand, afraid to push too hard on her skin.

A voice broke the silence, making me jump.

"Hello, I am Dr. Wraithsmith. You must be friends of Nicole." He wasn't wearing a gown or other protective gear.

"We are waiting for results to come back from her bloodwork. We don't know what she is infected with, but it is most likely a virus. Her biggest problem now, is that the virus has triggered something called DIC. Basically, the system of proteins in your blood that forms a clot when you cut yourself, is going haywire in her body, and she is clotting all over."

"But she's bleeding! Not clotting," I practically yelled at him.

"Yes, that's what happens. The body keeps clotting until it runs out of those clotting proteins. When it runs out, you can't clot at all, and you start bleeding. That's why she has blood in her eyes and ears. The red rash is her small blood vessels leaking into her skin.

"There is a certain sequence that your clotting factors normally follow. This situation is very unique. Unfortunately, there is not a lot we can do to stop it. We've started her on blood thinners, to help slow down the clotting. We've stabilized her breathing and her heart rate, but without knowing for sure that it's a virus, or what kind of virus it is, there isn't a lot more we can do right now."

Carl stood up and came toward us. "When will you know if it is a virus?"

Dr. Wraithsmith cleared his throat and shrugged. "We don't know. We've sent samples away for viral culture, but it can take a week to get results. Symptomatically, we can rule out the common ones - measles for example - and the onset was far too fast for something like ebola.

"The only reference I could find that fit the suddenness of her symptoms is from a very old infectious disease text describing a syndrome called the 'Bane of Erebus.' That text was written before we had the technology to culture and identify viruses, so I don't know the actual infectious agent. The text did note that it was typically introduced through a wound or bite," he nodded to Nicole's hand, "and that it did not appear to be easily transmitted through casual contact"

I groaned and turned my attention back to Nicole.

"Is she going to survive this?" Carl asked.

Dr. Wraithsmith cleared his throat again. "We are doing all we can to treat her condition and reduce her pain, but there is nothing else we can do for her aside from supportive care. We don't know enough about the virus, if that's what it is, to know how to fight it. It's up to her body to fight it off. I'm sorry, but with this rapid and advanced presentation, and not really knowing the cause, it's unlikely she will survive."

Carl nodded and walked Dr. Wraithsmith out of the room.

I knelt next to the bed and closed my eyes. Maybe I could help her another way. Maybe Dionysus would have an answer. I focused on sending my mind to the partition.

The grove appeared before me. I sat in my stone chair.

"Nicole, you can't leave me now, we just..." I wept.

A chair scraped along the floor of the gazebo. I looked up and saw Dionysus sitting across from me, like he had been waiting for me to come.

"The measures that your healers have taken to ease her pain will stop working soon. Her blood works against her. As her vessels fill with clots, she will lose feeling in her limbs, and eventually, her heart will stop being able to pump blood to her organs. Her body will shut down. She will struggle, she will fight, but eventually... she will fail." He put his hand on mine. "I am sorry you have to suffer this. I am here for you."

Through the fog, I could hear Nicole groan and cry from the increasing pain.

"Dionysus, can you help her? You healed my hand..."

He looked defeated. He straightened his back and shook his head. "I could enter her, and I could heal her. But the moment I left, she would experience excruciating pain as her body failed and she died. Only someone from a vessel bloodline can bring Gods in and survive."

I slammed my fist down on the table. "Then get in there and heal her!" I could barely focus on what he was saying. The fog vibrated with her screams of pain.

Dionysus calmly folded his hands. "Then we should get to work."

"What do I do then? Do I cut her hand? How can I get you into her? If death is inevitable, then the least we can do is end her suffering!"

Dionysus bowed his head in acknowledgment. "As you wish. Let me into you, cut your hand and drip some blood into her mouth. I will be channeled from your body to hers. I will heal her, then leave her body. I can do nothing more for her."

He sat back and looked at me, waiting for a decision.

"Alright, do I need to do the ritual again to summon you?" Dionysus leaned forward.

"No, I am here waiting to be let in. Just relax and say you welcome me. Like this - he stood and put his arms out to his side. "Dionysus I welcome you!" He sat down again. "Just like that."

I left the partition in a puff of foggy smoke.

I stood up and looked to Carl. Several nurses and Dr. Wraithsmith were standing by, looking dumbfounded, watching her scream. Empty syringes sat on a cart that wasn't in the room before.

"Carl?" I looked at him confused.

"They tried to put her into a coma, so she wouldn't feel the pain. It's not working." He said dejectedly.

"Carl, all of them need to go. Now."

The nurses and doctor looked at me, surprised. Carl motioned for them to leave, but they didn't budge. He looked to me and back to the medical staff.

"Can Mr. Anth have a little privacy please?"

They nodded and stepped down the hall. Carl moved into the doorway, putting his back to Nicole and me.

I relaxed my body and put out my hands to the side. "Dionysus, I welcome you." I whispered. My eyes were locked on Nicole. I wasn't going to let her leave this world without a witness. I would drag this memory through life to my grave. I deserved it.

The flash of bluish-white light was brief, far less vigorous than when I had first summoned him.

"Good, I am present but not in control. Cut your hand and drip a few drops of blood into her mouth."

I pulled my pocket knife out and cut my hand. The ring on my hand felt like molten fire. I dropped the knife on the table next to me and cupped her jaw in my hand. Her teeth were clenched, so I pursed her lips and squeezed a couple of drops between her lips. Each drop glowed and swirled with bluish energy and seemed to slide between her teeth with intention. I felt a deep **THUMP** in my chest as Dionysus passed from me to her. The cut on my hand remained open and bleeding.

"Carl, Dionysus is going to help her. She won't survive, but we won't let her suffer either. It won't be completely painless." My voice broke as I explained.

Carl turned and came to my side.

The red splotches on her skin faded, the bleeding from her orifices stopped, and color came back to her face. She looked weak, but she was no longer writhing in pain. She raised her hand up to me.

"Thank you, Dom. I-"

She started to convulse. Machines beeped and alarmed. The nurses and Dr. Wraithsmith came running back in. They looked shocked and confused. No longer lying weak and frail, instead Nicole seized and flailed with amazing strength. The nurses couldn't hold her down. Her face looked peaceful, but her body lurched and twisted in ways that made me sick. Her joints cracked as her limbs straightened and seized back and forth.

It was over as fast as it began. Her body went limp, and a steady tone rang out through the room. One of the nurses quickly turned it off. We all stared at her. She was clearly dead, though all signs of the virus had vanished. They respectfully started straightening her body, tucking the sheet around her like she was sleeping.

I felt my eyes burn with tears. I couldn't believe it was over. I hoped for a miracle. Several minutes passed in silence. I wiped my eyes and looked at Dr. Wraithsmith. He took off his gloves and tossed them in a garbage before coming over to me.

"I'm truly sorry for your loss. Do you have any information for her next of kin?

I nodded absently. "I'll call them. I've known her parents a long time."

I went back to the corner where my jacket lay tossed on a chair and grabbed my phone. The nurses were on their way out of the room. My vision was blurred, and my lungs didn't want to draw air. I pulled out my phone and sat down. I stared at Nicole for a second before dialing her parents' number.

Ring ring
Ring ring
Ring ring

"Hi, you've reached Thomas and Terri. We're not in right now. Please leave a message after the bark! **Grrarf!** *"*

"Hi, Mr. and Mrs. Fein. It's Domonic calling. Can you please call me back as soon as possible - it's an emergency... Bye."

Carl stood in the door.

"Domonic, they want to prepare Nicole to go downstairs. They want us out while they do that."

I stood up and went into the hall. One of the nurses came back to us.

"We have a quiet space where you can stay for a while" she said kindly, steering me gently by the back of my arm.

I turned to follow, but my legs gave out. I crumpled, and I slid down the wall, ending in a miserable puddle on the floor. I stared without seeing.

"What do I do, Carl? I'm not supposed to give in to what I'm feeling right? Is numb okay?"

Carl crouched next to me. "Yeah, numb is okay."

~

"Who are you?" Nicole was standing on a beach, surrounded by mist. A handsome man stood not too far from her.

"I am Dionysus. Domonic sent me to you to stop the pain. You will suffer from the virus no more."

Nicole realized she couldn't feel the pain anymore. Just a moment ago, she had felt like her blood was turning into sludge. Her chest had felt a weight like someone was sitting on it, and her skin had felt like it was going to melt off. Now she felt fine.

"Oh, thank you! I feel so much better! I... I. I feel..."

She felt dizzy. Her partition shook violently. Dionysus began to fade in front of her. He smiled as his form faded into a cloud of smoke, knowing that her suffering was nearing an end.

"Wait!" Nicole called out.

Dionysus's form snapped back into existence. He looked terrified.

"What is happening?"

"Don't leave me here! I don't know where I am."

"Nicole, I need you to let me go. You are dying. It is painful. It will only be a few seconds, but it will continue until I leave."

She looked at him in a panic. "What? Dying? But I feel better. What's happening?"

The world spun. Sand, rocks, and water shot in every direction, thrown out of the perimeter of her partition, until nothing remained. The spinning slowed, and they were floating, orbiting each other in the chaos.

"Nicole!" Dionysus opened his hands, reaching for her, panic on his face as darkness enveloped them both.

~

I watched the nurses go into Nicole's room, leaving the door slightly ajar.

"I never should have come back here. I should have just started trekking the world and ruining my own life. I never meant for her to get hurt."

Carl sat on the floor next to me. We sat in silence, and the ambient sounds of the hospital dwindled and faded as I brooded. Suddenly, my

267

skin prickled, and my heart skipped a beat when I heard the faint, familiar laughter.

"HA HA HA HAA HAAA!"

I bolted to my feet. Was he here?

"Domonic? What's wrong?" Carl stood.

"I heard him - Erebus. I just heard his laugh. He's not in me. No one is."

Carl put a hand on my shoulder. "I didn't hear anything. Where did it come from?"

"It was behind me -"

I realized from where I had heard it coming. I pushed past Carl.

"Nicole!"

I barged through the door. The nurses were washing the blood off her body. A large plastic bag was open next to her. They looked up at me, startled.

Did I imagine the laugh? My eyes scanned Nicole, then every corner of the room.

One of the nurses came toward me. "Sir, you must wait outside, please. You may see her when she's cleaned up and covered."

Carl pulled me back from the door. We walked down the hall, then he put his hands on my shoulders and turned my back to the wall.

"Domonic, come on. It's time to walk away from this. She's gone. She's not suffering anymore. You can grieve, but you have to-"

A blinding blue-white flash interrupted him. The sounds of air rushing past us raised the hair on the back of my neck. He dropped his arms and turned around. I couldn't breathe. We looked at each other, then bolted back to the room.

The nurses were laying on the floor, unconscious. Nicole was standing next to the bed. A piercing blue light shone from deep within her eyes, and her sheet had dropped to the floor, the basin of bloody water overturned and running to the floor drain.

"Carl, no kneeling this time?"

It was Dionysus. The timber of his voice was unmistakable.

"But… how!? You said she wouldn't survive!" My voice strained with confusion and relief I was feeling. My shoulders dropped. My stomach was filled with fire.

"And yet she has. It appears that she belongs to another bloodline capable of being a vessel. I, however, do not inhabit female vessels. Personal preference."

The light in her eyes faded. Carl caught her as she fell. He lifted her pale form back onto the bed and quickly wrapped the sheet around her. I stood there dumbly, watching him.

"We need to go." Carl said, easily throwing Nicole over his shoulder. "Domonic - MOVE!"

Carl and I left the room. We walked swiftly down the hallway to an exit sign. Behind us we could hear raised voices call out.

"We have code yellow! Call it in!"

Ahead of us were stairs leading down and hopefully out. We came across a door that had warning signs indicating that their fire alarms would sound if we went through them. Carl paused only for a moment before kicking the door open so hard that the handle hit the glass, cracking it.

We ran to the car, which Carl had parked in the nearby emergency parking.

"Domonic, you drive!" Carl ordered and tossed me the key.

I fumbled but caught it. He placed Nicole upright in the backseat then climbed in himself. I got in, started the car, and sped away.

Carl pulled out his phone and dialed.

"Mr. Donovan, there is a complication. I need you to call me back as soon as you get this message. Thank you."

I tried to look at them over my shoulder.

"Carl, how is she?"

"Eyes on the road, Domonic!"

The car swerved, and I repeated the question.

I looked at him in the rear-view mirror.

Carl looked up at me with an exasperated expression.

"I don't know! I'm not exactly a leading authority on divine healing. She's unconscious and breathing. We need to get her back to your place."

I drove. Carl kept checking his phone every few seconds. He let out a frustrated sigh.

"Domonic, there's another problem. If Nicole really is a vessel, there is a chance you two are closely related. And if that's the case, you two can never have children. That child would be a rampant vessel from the moment it takes its first breath."

"Well let's fucking hope not Carl. We did have sex just before she started bleeding everywhere!" I slammed my hand on the wheel.

We drove in silence. When we arrived, I helped Carl carry Nicole through the door and up the stairs. He laid her in bed, and I gently tucked her in. She looked better than before, there was some color back in her cheeks, although her breathing was weak and shallow. We left the room quietly

We sat in the living room in silent exhaustion.

"I need a drink!" Carl said. He got back up and headed into the kitchen.

"Carl, grab me a bottle too please?"

Carl examined the case of wine bottles. He held one up thoughtfully for a moment, then broke the seal on the bottle.

"I was told this stuff needs to breathe. Today it'll have to go without."

Carl opened another bottle and handed one to me. He took his own bottle to the couch.

"Carl, why didn't we keep her at the hospital?" I asked. My voice trembled. I was trying to stay calm, but my emotions teetered on the edge.

He looked over at me and took a long drink before answering.

"They hadn't had time to process her information. Everyone was certain she was going to die. That big flash, the unconscious nurses, not to mention her sudden miraculous recovery, those things draw attention. Attention

273

to you and to her. And that is the last thing you need in your life."

I stared at the wine bottle and then looked at him. I raised the bottle up.

"To you, to Dionysus, and to Nicole not being dead."

He raised his bottle and we drank.

~

"You knew she was a vessel, that's why you put the bite to her?" Dionysus looked at Erebus accusingly.

Erebus giggled "OF COURSE! IT WAS THE ONLY WAY SHE WOULD AWAKEN!"

Dionysus marveled at him. He turned his attention back to watering his grapes. They were about ready to be taken off the vine.

"Well, isn't this just delightful. Two of them so close together - this could be fun!"

Erebus tried to contain his laughter. He bit down on his fingers.

"What is so funny about all of this?"

Erebus shook his head, grinning, and vanished.

"Well little grapes, today has been interesting."
He continued down the line. "I think the other
families are going to be very interested in her
when they find out."

Dionysus saw the blur of something flying
through the air in his peripheral vision. He
turned to see Ares standing at the edge of the
vineyard.

"Hello brother. What can I do for you?"

Ares entered the grove and walked alongside
Dionysus. His tremendous body was easily
twice the Dionysus' size.

"What has Erebus been doing here? So often I
sense him, and it is making my skin crawl."

Ares plucked a grape and ate it. It was tart and
sweet with a fiery undertone. His face cracked
with a massive smile.

"Brother, you truly are gifted."

Dionysus couldn't help but smile. He was proud of his beautiful grapes. He tilted his head to look at Ares.

"You are familiar with the vessel bloodline that is bonded to us?"

Ares looked around to ensure Erebus was not hiding and listening. Satisfied that they were alone, he turned back to Dionysus.

"Yes, of course, what about them?"

He reached for another grape and plucked it. Rolling it around in his hand, he waited patiently.

"The current heir found another bloodline. There are two vessels now." Dionysus said, gently setting his watering can down. He turned to see Ares smiling as he popped another grape into his mouth.

"Another bloodline survived the war?" Ares frowned. "I thought the Magus's had hunted them all down during the Meggido conflict?"

Dionysus shrugged and examined another vine. "I was led to believe so as well brother. Yet, she lives."

Ares' face lit up. He started chewing another grape. He wiped some juice from his chin before speaking again.

"Well, the others will be delighted another vessel has been awoken."

As quickly as he had come, he leapt into the distance, leaving a faint smoky trail in his wake.

"They most certainly will be." Dionysus sighed and looked out across his vineyard. "Too many visitors. My precious little things relax now. They are all gone."

~

"That's good wine." Carl remarked.

He set the empty bottle down and stretched out on the couch. I sat in my chair, finishing my own bottle, lost in my thoughts. *Nicole, I should have never gone to my uncle's funeral. I was too curious. Damn the money, damn my 'inheritance.' I'd give it all up if I could undo what has been done to you.*

The silence was broken by a sharp knock on the door.

"I'm not expecting anyone…" Carl stood quickly. He reached inside his jacket and moved to unholster his pistol. He went up to the door and looked through the peephole, then holstered his weapon and let out a relieved sigh. "It's Eric."

I looked at him with an eyebrow raised. "Mr. Donovan? That was fast."

Carl opened the door.

"Carl, thank you. Sorry, I missed your call. I was just getting into town." He came through the door and looked around, then dropped his travel case on the table. "Why does it smell like depression and alcohol in here?" he looked pointedly at me.

We told him everything. He sat and listened, eyes widening as the details were unraveled.

"This is incredible. You certainly dove head first into the shallow end lad. It's a damn miracle she is alive." Mr. Donovan stood up and went to his travel case. He took out his laptop and started typing away furiously.

"First, I'm going to make sure you two are not related. As far as I knew, you were the last vessel. This complicates matters." Eric worked with incredible focus and intensity. After a few minutes, he closed his laptop and stepped into the hall. Carl and I impatiently waited for him to return. We could hear his muffled voice echo through the door.

"I'm sure it'll be alright. You two don't look anything alike." Carl tried for some levity, but it didn't do much to lift my spirits. My head dropped into my hands, and Carl sighed.

"I'm just happy she's alive, Carl. If we're cousins or something, I can live with her just being alive." I raised my head and looked at him with a tight-lipped smile. "What a fucking nightmare." My voice broke, and I dropped my head back into my hands.

Eric came in and closed the door. He had a big smile on his face. "Good news! There is no way you two are related."

I let out a tremendous sigh of relief. I stood up and shook Eric's hand, then turned back to Carl.

Behind him, Nicole was standing in the door, wrapped in a blanket.

"That's good. After what we did, I would hate to be related." She said with a weak laugh.

I rushed over and hugged her. She held on tightly. Carl came up toward us, examining Nicole's face.

"Nicole, how are you feeling?" I asked as holding onto her.

She pulled back and tilted her head up to face me. She smiled warmly at me, then Carl and Eric. She hugged me even tighter.

"I feel fantastic Dom, just... fantastic. So, I'm a vessel?"

I bobbed my head in acknowledgement and laughed.

"Yeah! I guess so."

"I wonder which Gods are going to visit me…" She mused. "I guess we have some choices to make about where we're going to go, and what we're going to do."

We kissed. I was content that fate had not managed to tear us apart.

We were barely aware of Eric's phone ringing.

"Hello? Yes, this is Eric Donovan." I could feel Eric's mood change, like a palpable shift in the room.

"Eric? Is everything alright?"

Eric leaned on the table, one hand pressed flat and the other held his phone to his head tightly.

He ignored me. "I understand, yes. Goodbye." He dropped his phone to the floor and took a deep, ragged breath. He turned to me, then his gaze held Carl's.

"Domonic, that- I- I was their emergency contact. They didn't know who they were. It took them time."

Eric closed his eyes, took another slow, deep breath, steadying himself.

I let go of Nicole and walked over to Eric, gently setting a hand on his shoulder. "Eric, what's happened?"

Eric opened his eyes. "Your parents. Their plane went down near Williamsport, Indiana. They're alive, but we need to go. The CDC is on site, and they said something about a quarantine. Your parents are asking for you. Carl, start the car. You two, pack your bags. We have to leave right now."

End of Book One of the Pantheon War Trilogy.

Find out what happens next in Book Two of the
Pantheon War Trilogy "God Heads"

Special Thanks

This book wouldn't have been possible without the ongoing assistance from the following people. Thank you, all of you.

Konra Mueller
Travis Hulstein
Sylvia Rothwell
Kenneth Maclean
David Waltz
Eric Young
Calvin Adams
David Zeeb

About the Author

Daniel was born and raised in southern Alberta, he has worked in a variety of fields, at the time of writing this book he is working as a Systems Administrator. This is his first published work made available to everyone.

Please, take a finger, toe, or nose and press it against this dot for three seconds.

Thank you!

You can contact Daniel by email at
daniel.j.ward@outlook.com